Drifting To Glory

Copyright ©1999. Richard Danforth Sherlock. All rights reserved. No part of this material may be reproduced in any form without permission from the editors, except for reviews in periodicals.

Library of Congress Cataloging-in-Publication Data

ISBN 1-889332-44-5

Heritage Press
1318 Burton Valley Rd.
Nashville, TN 37215-4306

Cover Photo: Bucktail Monument, Gettysburg, PA. The Maltese Cross was the Fifth Corp Badget in the Army of the Potomac to which the Bucktails belonged.

Drifting To Glory

by
Richard Danforth Sherlock

*To my dear wife, Gerri,
who patiently endured my absence
at the typewriter in my study,
and helped me with her
very good suggestions and criticisms.*

*Also to the memory of my son, Kenneth,
who would have enjoyed the story.*

July 1913 – 50th Anniversary Battle of Gettysburg
Driftwood, PA

Byron Danforth
2nd from Right, 2nd Row from Rear.

PROLOGUE

During early spring of 1938, a group of people met to discuss the re-enactment of a river raft trip which was made in 1861. Several of the group were descendants of the famous Pennsylvania "Bucktail" Regiment of Civil War fame. The purpose of the re-enactment was to honor the memory of those brave men who had originally made the two hundred mile journey to enlist in the aid of their country. They had drifted down the Susquehanna River to offer their services to the governor at the state capital at Harrisburg.

The "last raft," as it was called, was built by expert woodsmen and was 120 feet long. It had a small shanty, or cabin, near the middle of the raft.

The passengers included several women and a few other interested people who had helped to sponsor the undertaking. The crew consisted of experienced raftsmen and rivermen including Harry Conner, a veteran river pilot. Also aboard was W. C. Proffitt, a Universal Newsreel cameraman who planned to record the trip on film.

The raft departed west of Williamsport, Pa. on March 19, 1938, and had negotiated the most dangerous section of the river on March 20 when it passed the Williamsport Dam. More passengers were picked up at Market Street at Williamsport. The total on board was now forty-eight.

After they departed, the raft swung around the river bend north of Muncy, Pa. About a mile south of the Muncy-Montgomery highway bridge, the raft was to pass under a railroad bridge. The raft swerved in the current as it approached the bridge. The bow hit the fifth span of the bridge, swinging the stern into the sixth span. Crew and passengers were thrown into the cold water, including the Newsreel cameraman who took pictures until the collision. As a result of the accident, the chief pilot was drowned. Six others were missing including the cameraman. Not all of the bodies were recovered until after dark. The remainder of those who had been on board were saved by the quick action of local residents. A Boy Scout boat and other small craft picked up some of the struggling survivors. People along the shore also helped in the rescue efforts.

In spite of the tragedy, the remaining crew and passengers elected to continue the trip to Harrisburg. They intended to present a trophy to the governor commemorating the original raft trip. They were determined to continue in the tradition of raftsmen who did not abandon a project, even with the loss of life.

By mid morning, the fog had lifted sufficiently to allow the raftsmen to untie the lines and push off.

Interested observers cheered from the bridges and shoreline. According to the <u>Williamsport Gazette and Bulletin,</u> an estimated ten thousand cars had arrived in the Muncy area during the previous afternoon and evening. Small boats followed along, making quite a flotilla.

As the raft neared a little village called White Deer, the fog still shrouded areas of the river and shoreline. In the interest of safety, the raft was eased toward the shore, temporarily. One of the crew, Josh Harrington, thought he noticed some people through the fog and reeds. He spoke to his brother, Delmar, and one of the sponsors, Mrs. St. John. "Do you see those three men?" He pointed to a light area in the fog. "They look like they're wearing old Civil War uniforms with bucktails on their caps. Don't you see them?" His friends agreed they saw something, but the fog thickened again. Others in the group said the visibility was too poor to discern anything clearly. They saw only shadows as the sun broke in and out of the scuddy clouds. Josh stared intently through a small break in the fog and saw the figures again. They seemed to be beckoning the raftsmen to approach the shore as if they wanted to come aboard for the trip.

The new pilot, Richard Post, decided to have the raft poled through the reeds and up against the shore, if, for no other reason, to await better visibility in which to continue. He was intent on preventing any additional accidents.

They pushed through the reeds and up against the sandy shore. Josh and others shouted, "Hello, anybody there? Come along if you want to join us. We're leaving as soon as the fog lifts!" There was no response. The only sound they could hear was the water lapping against the sides of the raft. A bright sun broke through the wispy clouds and fog as the raftsmen walked along the shore for several yards in both directions. They found footprints in the soft dirt, but could not be sure who had made them. They appeared to be recent. It was very quiet, almost eerie, and a number of the men and women had a strangely uncomfortable feeling about the scene. They spoke quietly about it.

In about half an hour the cloud cover and visibility had improved considerably. Mr. Post directed the raft to be poled into the current, and they were underway once more. The front and rear oarsmen took their positions.

The crew and passengers chatted about the sightings of the three Bucktails as they drifted down river. Several of the men who had seen nothing laughed about it and teased those who thought they had seen something. A few superstitious men cleared an area near the stern of the raft. One man said, "Here is a place where our three visitors can sit undisturbed. They can enjoy the voyage with us."

The men and women continued their journey drifting down the Susquehanna in the bright sunshine. Those people who knew what they had seen talked about it in hushed tones and wondered about the incident. They knew they would remember it vividly and would relate it to others for the rest of their lives.

Chapter I

I arose early as usual. The wooden floor was cold and I hated leaving my warm comfortable bed. In addition to a flannel nightshirt, I had worn my woolen socks to help keep my feet warm.

The weather in western New York state can be very cold and irritating in April. Winter dies hard there. The Great Lakes area is a weather factory and spawns late winter storms that swing across the area, dumping as much snow as quickly as possible on us. I thought of the winter as I washed my hands and face at the basin on the night stand. On the coldest winter mornings, it was not unusual to find a soft layer of ice in the pitcher. Thank goodness no ice today.

Dressing quickly, I blew out the lamp and hurried down stairs to find mother preparing breakfast. The pleasant aroma of bacon, eggs, and coffee filled the large kitchen.

"Good morning, mamma. I wasn't very hungry until I smelled your cooking, but now I could eat a bear. Is father up yet?" I said, yawning and stretching.

"Good morning, By. No, I don't think he's awake, but he will be quickly…soon as he gets a whiff of this strong coffee. He'll roll out when he realizes there's food ready."

Mother always called me "By." She ordinarily called me Byron only on those occasions when she was angry with me. My father tended to follow the same practice.

Father finally descended the stairs and entered the kitchen hoisting his suspenders over his shoulders. "Good morning all. Hope everyone slept well. You have everything smelling almost good enough to eat, Mary," he said, smiling. He put his arm around her, pulling her to his side and kissed her on the cheek. She was a little woman, only as tall as his shoulder since he was six feet tall. The Danforth men were all taller than average.

I added some wood to the stove and sat at the table. I realized how much my father had aged over the past few months. I noticed something else, too, and smiled as I spoke. "You know father, I'm sure this sounds strange since I'm nineteen now, but I've just realized we don't look much alike. I thought we did when I was a lad, but now you have dark hair and brown eyes. I have mother's light brown hair and blue eyes. I agree our sharp noses and chins are alike. Guess you don't think about some things 'till you're older."

Father laughed. "Well, I'm your old man unless your mother knows something I don't." He chuckled as he sat down, sipping his first cup of strong black coffee.

Mother looked at him with her hands on her hips, a slight frown appearing on her face. "John, you know darn well By is your son. Don't pay any mind to him, By. He must need more rest. It's too early for that kind of humor."

My sisters were giggling over what my folks had said as they helped with the cooking. My oldest sister – Electa was twenty-three. The middle daughter – Mary was twenty-one, and the youngest child – Abigail was fifteen. Abbie was my favorite. She flitted about the large kitchen setting the table for the family. That was one of her tasks, and she enjoyed placing everything correctly.

As I was eating, I looked at my father and asked, "What do you think of all the war talk, father? It seems to be the main topic of conversation around here, lately."

He looked at me for a moment and could tell I was very serious. "Well, By, I can't put too much stock in it. There have been disagreements between north and south for years, and they have always been able to work out their problems without shooting at one another."

"Yeah, I know it," I said, "but it appears to be getting much more serious every time you pick up the newspaper from Olean. I'm just the right age if it comes to a shooting war, and I have thoughts both ways as to what I should do if it comes down to that. It would be a tough decision for me to make. My buddy Cliff thinks he would enlist right away, but it bothers me. I hope I won't be forced to decide."

"Oh, Mr. Young would probably shoot Cliff first if he tried to enlist and save an enemy the trouble," father answered. "I think we all need to be patient, and cross that bridge when we get to it." I noticed him exchanging worried looks with mother.

As we finished eating, the girls cleared the table. Abbie collected her books and got ready to go to school. She came over to me and said, "Don't you worry, By. If they come to take you off to war, I'll hide you way back in the woods."

I laughed and hugged her. "You're a sweetheart, Abbie. Hurry off to school before you're late."

"Well, I'll get on with my chores," I said. I tried to forget about the war talk, but the thought stayed with me. My work consisted of helping my father manage the operation of the Danforth Inn where the family lived in Ceres, N.Y. In addition to the family quarters, we had eight guest rooms which the girls kept clean.

The feature of the inn which we enjoyed most was the wide covered porch that extended across the front. There were flower pots along the front railing which the girls took pride in keeping full of petunias and pansies. A line of spiraea bushes below the railing decorated the porch. They were covered with buds, and the white blossoms would be beautiful before long.

I enjoyed having fun with the guests at the inn. I would tell them that I could stand on the front steps of the porch and throw a stone from New York to Pennsylvania. Then, I'd laugh and tell them that this was not too difficult since the Pennsylvania line was only fifty yards from the inn.

I worked at the inn all during my school years, but now I thought I'd like to see what else the world had to offer. My folks would have been happy for me to spend the rest of my life with them, but I could not envision doing that.

After completing my morning work, I decided to visit my school chums, Ed Dodd and Cliff Young. They were both working at the sawmill on the edge of town.

It was a gorgeous April day. The temperature was rising and the trees were showing their first delicate green leaves. The warm sun was promoting growth everywhere. Crocus and lilies were appearing in the yards. Birds were busy building nests in the shrubs and trees along the street. I could not have been happier in the beauty of the day.

As I passed the Dodd home, I saw Ed's mother hanging her washing at the clothesline. "You won't have any trouble drying that wash today, Mrs. Dodd," I said, waving to her.

"Not in this nice warm breeze," she replied. "By, if you're walking as far as the mill, would you do me a favor and take Ed's lunch to him? He left in a hurry this morning and ran off without it."

"Glad to do it. I'm heading that way." As I walked across the field to the mill, I saw Ed and Cliff loading planks on a wagon at the side of the mill. I hollered at them. "I've brought the lunch so we can all eat now." Ed knew whose lunch it was, and thanked me for bringing it. Cliff sat down in the shade of the wagon and began to eat.

While they ate, I looked at them and said, "Can't help noticing how fit you guys look. This kind of work must be keeping you in good shape. Hard labor evidently agrees with you."

Cliff smiled. "You know, By, I'm up to about one eighty five...mostly muscle." He winked at Ed who just shook his head and went on eating. "Yeh, at six-two I don't look that heavy. Although you're twenty pounds lighter, or so; at six feet, we still could pass for brothers...same eyes and hair, except I'm a little more on the handsome side, wouldn't you say?" Ed pretended to choke on his food and laughed. Ed was the smallest of the trio, and enjoyed the way we always kidded each other. He had dark hair and eyes and was quite muscular.

When they had finished their lunch, Cliff said, "Now that the formalities are out of the way, to what do we owe the honor of this visit?"

"Oh, I've been talking to my dad, pondering what may happen before long if those southern states continue with this secession business, and what it could mean to all of us. It troubles me every time I think about it, and I've been thinking about it a lot lately.

"Tell you what," Cliff said. "Ed and I will come over this evening after supper, and we can jaw about it. Maybe we can ease your mind a little."

That evening I sat on the front porch petting the family dog, a little year old beagle. Cliff and Ed arrived and pulled up chairs next to me, one on either side. They put their feet on the porch railing. I smiled and said, "I hope you guys are comfortable."

Ed laughed. "Yes, we're just dandy...always like to make ourselves at home."

Cliff smiled, saying, "Now we want to try to make you a little more comfortable about what you were saying about a possible war. Ed and I were talking on the way over here. We think we have figured out what may be bothering you. We think it's not knowing what's going to happen, you know, fear of the unknown. We believe if a war is forced on us, that you'll realize enlisting with us is the patriotic thing to do. You'd feel strange staying at home with the women when most of the young bucks in the county are gone."

"Of course staying at home with the women when most of the men are gone could have some advantages," Ed chortled.

Cliff and I both had to laugh at that thought. "You're probably right, Cliff, and if we have to go, I can't think of two men I'd rather be with than you two. You know what really sticks in my craw, though? If war comes, we will be fighting our own countrymen – not some foreign country like Mexico or France. The enemy will be guys just like us who speak the same language and love this land like we do." Cliff and Ed paused as they thought about what I had said.

Ed answered, saying, "The difference is this, By. Those southern states that are trying to leave the union want to break this country into two smaller ones, and they have convinced their young men that they may have to kill a bunch of us in order to do it. It has passed the talking stage with them. Also, this business of slavery is an issue that will only end with bloodshed."

I nodded and said, "What you say makes sense. I wonder what it must be like to shoot a man and see him drop, knowing that you were the one responsible for his death? I can't say I'm thrilled by the idea."

Cliff spoke up, trying to encourage me a little. "Well, we've sure shot our share of deer in Allegany county. I remember after the first one; it was much easier. Shooting a man must be something like that."

"Remember, too," I answered, "those deer were not shooting back! That made it easier, too." They laughed at my logic. "None of us have ever been very far from home," I continued, "and if we have to go, it would be a good chance to see some of the country. If war comes and it's as short as they say it will be, we won't be gone more than a few months." I looked at my friends and wondered how much truth there would be in what I had said.

Drifting To Glory

Chapter II

The next day as I sat on the steps of the inn, I was impressed by the stillness of the morning. It was eerily quiet with a gray overcast sky. As I looked up into the branches of the oak tree near the front porch, I noticed there was not a leaf moving, not even the hint of a breeze. It was so silent I thought I heard a horse galloping far off in the distance. The sound faded at first, and then I heard it again. In a few moments, I saw a horse and rider charging down the street toward me, creating a small cloud of dust. The horseman was covered with a gray powder-like dust, and his horse was lathered and foaming at the mouth.

I ran across the street where the rider had dismounted in front of the general store. He let his mount drink at the horse trough. Before the rider could speak, he drank from a tin cup of water the proprietor offered him. Several customers came out of the store, and they were joined by people on the street who formed a small crowd around the stranger.

"What's all the hurry about, sir," I asked. I had an uneasy feeling that I already knew his answer.

Between gulps of water the man said, "It's war! I've just ridden from Olean, and the Pennsy Railroad telegraph operator got the message. The Southerners have attacked Fort Sumter, and President Lincoln has called for volunteers along with the regular army. I'm on my way home, trying to inform as many folks along my way as I can. Gotta get going…God bless President Lincoln!"

I watched the rider disappear as quickly as he had arrived. I felt my stomach tighten and knew I'd have to make up my mind about the war very soon.

We learned in a day or two that hostilities had begun on April 13, 1861, and by April 18th, I stood in front of the store reading the recruiting announcement. Cliff and Ed were with me.

VOLUNTEER RIFLES!
MARKSMEN WANTED!

"By Authority of Governor Curtin, a company will be formed this week of citizens of McKean and Elk counties, who are prepared to take arms immediately, to support the Constitution of the United States and defend the Commonwealth of Pennsylvania. I am authorized to accept at once for service any man who will bring in with him to my headquarters a rifle which he knows how to use. Come forward Americans who are not degenerate from the spirit of 76! Come forward in time to save the city of Washington from capture – in time to save the flag of the Union there from being humbled as it has been at Fort Sumter.

Smethport, April 17, 1861   THOMAS L. KANE

Headquarters at the Bennett House, Smethport. Muster Roll at the same place, and questions answered. Apply without further notice."

As we finished reading the poster, I spoke to my friends. "Well, I guess this is our opportunity to step forward and be counted. I've thought about it, prayed about it, talked to my folks about it and with you two guys. I'm sure we'll be doing the right thing and our patriotic duty by signing up. I can be ready when you guys are, so hurry up and get a move on before I change my mind. Hell, let's give it a try!"

"By, we knew you'd come around to seeing it our way," Cliff said. "We'll get busy and wind up things here, and maybe we can leave in a day or two."

"We might even recruit a few more to go with us," Ed added. "We won't have much extra time, though, with all we'll have to do to get ourselves ready."

I asked Cliff, "What did your boss at the sawmill have to say when you told him you and Ed were joining up?"

"Oh, he's a patriotic old cuss…fought in the Mexican War. He thinks we are doing the right thing and says he can get by without us for the two or three months we'll be gone."

"Yeah, he thinks he can get some older men to fill in while we are saving the Union for him," Ed said as he saluted. "I believe he'll be glad to be rid of us for a while. We have too much fun while we work. I understand from what my dad told us last night, most of the young men in Olean are forming companies and plan to leave as soon as possible."

At home that evening, I told my parents about my decision. "I think you have guessed that I've made up my mind to enlist with Cliff and Ed."

"We figured you would be going," father said. "Can't say I blame you. I'd probably do the same thing at your age."

Mother looked apprehensive as she spoke. "We just hope you'll be safe and will come home in a few weeks, By. Everyone seems to think that the government will make the Southerners come to terms, quickly."

"I hope so, mother. We're planning on it."

She looked at me and smiled, saying, "Before you boys leave, I understand there is going to be a dinner for you at the town hall and some dancing afterward. You boys better round up some girl friends in a hurry if you expect to have one available to spend the evening with."

As we proceeded to get our affairs in order, I wondered if there were other men who felt as I did at first. Surely, there must be others who are perplexed about what to do. I can think of one of our schoolmates who might fall in that group. I'll pay him a visit.

That afternoon I rode my horse, Buck, northwest to the little settlement of Portville, N.Y. It was a very pleasant five mile ride in the warm weather. Fluffy clouds drifted from the west, and just for a moment I thought it would be tempting to keep on going and ride out of the troublesome war situation altogether. Where would I go, and what would people think of me for disappearing at such a crucial time? I saw my friend's home and my mind drifted back to the business at hand.

Alex Chamberlain was not at home, but his mother directed me to the tannery where he worked. I thanked her and rode off. I didn't really need the directions because I could smell the foul odor of the tannery a half mile before I trotted up to the place. All I had to do was follow my nose. I don't think there is a more obnoxious stench than that emitted by a tannery. Even my horse snorted as we approached. "You don't like the air do you, Buck," I said, rubbing his neck as I tied him up.

I found Alex stretching some hides between frames in the back of the building. "Well, old buddy, I see you are hard at it here. You must be paid very well to put up with the stink. An outhouse smells like a rose compared with this."

"Well, how are you, By...haven't crossed your path in a while. Really, the smell is not bad once you get used to it. It's like living next to the railroad tracks. Pretty soon you get used to all the noise and don't hear the trains. What brings you to Portville? Come out to the pump and get a good drink of water. It won't taste near as bad as it smells around here."

"I'm just curious about what your thoughts are about the war. I'm going to enlist with Cliff Young and Ed Dodd, and we thought you might want to go with us. We'd be glad to have you along. They don't expect it to be a long war."

Alex smiled. "That's what I hear, but I thought I might wait to see if the fracas wouldn't be over and done with in that short time they think it will last. I really am tired of this work and the area. I've almost made up my mind to quit this job and enlist, too."

"I can understand wanting to leave this place," I said. "If you decide to do it, there's a party tomorrow in Ceres at seven o'clock, to be held in honor of all of us who are leaving. Hope you can come and bring a girl. Good seeing you again, Al."

"Same to you, By. I'll probably show up. So long."

I watched as Alex returned to work...his hands stained brown from tannic acid. Surely, army work couldn't be worse. He was slightly taller than me, with black hair and dark eyes...what the girls called handsome. I mounted up and was glad to ride out of range of the tannery.

When we saw the crowd that showed up for the dinner party, we were pleasantly surprised. Flags were hanging outside the town hall. Inside they had draped red, white, and blue bunting around the walls and across the room. There were spring flowers hanging from pots on the walls and on all the tables. The serving tables were filled with chicken, beef, and venison. There was no end to the vegetables, bread, pies, and cakes. I was both proud and hungry!

Everyone was spruced up for the occasion. The women and girls wore their prettiest ruffled gowns, and the men their Sunday suits. I hoped the new boots I wore would be broken in enough to be able to dance.

Before we ate, the preacher and mayor both made appropriate remarks for the occasion. Those of us who were to go off to the war were asked to stand. We were embarrassed when everyone applauded and were happy to sit down to eat.

I had been keeping company with Karen Heidenreich since my school days, and we ate together at the dinner. Karen was a petite, attractive girl of German descent.

Cliff and Ed had brought their girlfriends, and I was pleased that Alex had arrived with a girl from Portville. We ate at the same table, enjoying the food and conversation.

We danced after supper and my boots didn't bother me, but Karen winced a time or two.

The evening passed too quickly for everyone, and the town officials persuaded the musicians to stay longer. Even though the evening was cool, we warmed up as we square danced and waltzed around the hall. The boys changed partners often, in order to dance with as many girls as possible. The girls seemed to enjoy the variety, too.

I had always been somewhat distracted by the gowns the women wore, especially while growing into manhood. It seems oddly amusing to me that women are very careful to make sure their dresses are long enough to hide their legs, with perhaps just a little ankle showing. On the upper end, however, they have a lack of material to the extent that their breasts are quite generously revealed. Some of the more daring women seem to wear gowns that, on occasion, expose all of their breasts! I wonder if they do this on purpose, especially if they are quite voluptuous. Surely they know what they are showing. I'm slightly ashamed to be thinking of such things, but it is an uplifting, titillating thought.

I turned away, smiling, as I noticed a very large breasted woman, not far away, leaning over to pick up her handkerchief.

Drifting To Glory

Chapter III

A few of the local boys decided to join the New York State regiments, but when we discussed it, I thought we should make the trip to Smethport, Pa. There we would enlist with the regiment being formed by Thomas Kane, the man who signed the recruiting poster. Kane was from a prominent family, and we had read all his articles in the newspapers on the abolition of slavery. His father was a district judge, and his brother had been an arctic explorer. I suggested he would be a good man to serve under even though he had no military background. My friends agreed with me. We would enlist as Pennsylvania troops.

The day before we were to leave, we dawdled on the porch of the inn making small talk about the war, horses, guns and girls…not necessarily in that order. We were all jittery and decided we would break up early so we could spend our last evening at home with our families and girlfriends.

I said, "You know, I liked the way Mr. Kane put it on the poster when he wrote, 'Come forward Americans who are not degenerate from the spirit of 76,' and, 'bring a rifle you know how to use.' That's my kind of patriotism."

"I imagine he'll get all the recruits he can handle," Cliff replied, "and I hope they can all use their rifles!"

"And we'll be charter members of the regiment," Ed said.

We shook hands saying we'd see each other at daybreak.

I stayed up late chatting with my folks. The next thing I knew, mother was shaking me gently. "It's that time, By."

We assembled with all our gear in front of the inn. A blood red sun was just peeking over the hills in the east as father drove a wagon around from the barn behind the inn. The wagon was big enough for us four recruits and our gear. My dad had a good team hitched up, including my horse, Buck. Dad planned to drive us to Smethport, returning the next day. A few of the other recruits from the area planned to ride their own horses. My father told them he would lead their mounts back home, tied behind his wagon.

Knowing this, Alex asked, "If we are leaving the horses at Smethport, how are we going to get to our training camp?"

It was a reasonable question, but I thought I'd have a little fun with him. Acting like a preacher, I put my hand in the air and said, "Oh my son, you must trust in divine providence to lead you." Everyone laughed including Alex, and I added, "Seriously, Al, I suppose we'll do some marching to the nearest railhead somewhere, and take the train to the point where they'll train us. We'll know pretty soon."

A number of relatives and townspeople arrived to see us depart, even though it was just after daybreak. I said, "You would think we were heading for Washington instead of just twenty-eight miles to Smethport." I hugged my mother, sisters, and Karen who had come to say goodbye. The other boys bid farewell to their loved ones, and tears began to flow, especially not knowing when we would all meet again.

As we climbed up on the wagon, I said, "Thanks for coming out at such an early hour. We plan to make you proud of us and hope to be back in a few weeks."

The preacher was in the group and wished us God's speed and safe campaigning.

The mayor presented us with a new flag, which we attached to a pole at the back of the wagon. We cheered and waved our caps as the wagon lurched forward. The crowd cheered and clapped their hands and waved farewell.

One old Mexican War veteran hollered, "Shoot some of those Confederates for me, boys!" Just for a second I remembered the seriousness behind our departure, and a chill came over me that was not due to the early April morning.

"Don't you feel better now that we're on the road, and out of sight of our folks?" Cliff said.

"Yeah, I do," Ed agreed. "I think when folks leave home, it's always harder on those who stay behind."

The sun came out brightly enroute to Smethport, illuminating the new tree leaves, freshly plowed fields, and new flowers. The heady fragrance of honeysuckle and spring blossoms permeated the air. "A blind man could tell it was spring," I said. "Everything is really bright and clean. Mother nature adds a special sweetness to the air in spring," I said, looking across the landscape.

As we arrived in the little village of Eldred, Pa., we stopped by a creek to let the horses drink. A little boy playing in the water with his friend looked at us and asked, "Where are you folks going?"

"Well, we're on our way to join the army to fight for our country," I answered, smiling down at the lad.

"Wow! I wish I was older than ten, and I'd try to go with you," he replied. "Wait here until I can tell my mom." He turned and raced down the street, bare feet pattering in the dust. His younger companion was right behind him.

We laughed, thinking he was going to try to talk his mother into becoming a drummer boy. In a few minutes the boys were back with a pretty young woman. They carried a platter of cookies and a pitcher of milk.

"This is my mom and she just finished these cookies and wants you soldiers to have some," the ten year old said.

My father spoke up, saying, "Why, thank you, Ma'am, for your kindness. We appreciate the refreshment, don't we boys?"

"Yes, Ma'am," everyone said in unison.

"We picked a fine place to stop to rest," I added.

The lady smiled. "We will pray for your safe return," she said. She and the boys waved as we turned the horses back on the road and continued south.

Late in the afternoon, we began to see the buildings, a mile or so ahead, as Smethport came into view. Cliff said, "I hope they have supper cooking. The lunch our folks packed us, and the cookies and milk are beginning to wear off."

"Yeah, all this campaigning is building quite an appetite," Alex said, patting his stomach.

We laughed at him, and then made a turn in the road and entered the town. We spotted the Bennett house with no difficulty. It was an old two story building with a front porch. "Looks a lot like our inn doesn't it, father," I said.

"Yes, it does, except it's longer and fancier with the trim around the windows. They've improved it some since I saw it years ago," father replied.

As we pulled up where we were to rendezvous, a young man wearing military pants and a civilian shirt waved at us and approached the wagon.

He said, "I'm here to help you settle in. You can pick up a tent at the back of the house and pitch it anywhere you can find space...probably over there." He pointed to a grove of trees where other white tents were standing. He added, "Just flop the tent down there for now, and you can go get some chow where you see those tables set up. You can tie the horses to the right of the tents. There's feed and water for them there."

"Thanks for the help, friend. We are hungry," I said.

Ed had been driving when we arrived, so he moved the team and wagon over by the trees. We unloaded our gear, spread the tent over belongings, and made a beeline for the supper area. Beef stew, beans, bread, and coffee made a tasty meal for us in the open air. To top it off, the local ladies had prepared pies and cakes for dessert. Nothing was wasted.

"This soldiering is starting off pretty good so far, I think," Cliff said.

I had to agree and said, "Yes, sir, and maybe the regular army will wrap up the hostilities before we have to leave this picnic atmosphere, and we can turn around and go home. Nothing better than a good short war, I always say."

Father looked at me, smiled, nodded, but didn't speak as he finished his coffee.

"We'll be sorry to see you leave in the morning, Mr. Danforth," Alex said, as we set up our tent. "I know I speak for all of us when I say that we appreciate you helping us drive down here."

"Oh, I enjoyed the trip, boys," father answered. "I hope your induction goes smoothly and that you can all stay together after your training."

We built a small fire next to our tent and sat around talking for over an hour. The night was cool and clear with a sky peppered with stars. I said, "I guess I'm too excited to hit the hay, yet. I know we've all had a full day. Fatigue finally began to overtake us, and one by one we bid each other goodnight and crawled into the wall tent.

I thought I had only been asleep for a few minutes when the recruit encampment was rudely disturbed by reveille, beaten on a drum. It was six o'clock.

Cliff said, "What the hell was all that racket?"

I laughed and rubbed my eyes. "Oh, that's just the way they're going to tell us 'good morning' from now on, guys," I said as I sat up. "They'll wake us with a bugle as soon as someone joins up who has one."

While we were eating our breakfast, consisting of bacon, ham and eggs, a messenger passed by each table. He informed us that Col. Kane would be speaking to us at eight o'clock on the porch of the Bennett House.

"Father, why don't you stay until the colonel talks to us?" I said. "You could leave right after he speaks."

"I guess I can stay that long," he replied. "I would like to hear what he has to say to you boys. I'll still get home before dark."

"Let's all walk over to the porch right now," I said. "I want to be able to hear his speech. You miss half the words when you stand way in the back."

"Yeah, and we can get a good look at him, too," Cliff said. "Someone said he has a very stern appearance."

Promptly at eight o'clock our new commanding officer walked up on the porch. He was a tall, erect man, wearing a new uniform with the insignia of a Lieutenant Colonel and a broad brimmed officer's hat. Everything about him was impressive. His hair was black and hung in waves down to his collar. He had a full beard and moustache, and as he looked out at us, those of us up close could see his dark, piercing eyes. He was slim but well proportioned and was the perfect example of what I thought an officer should look like.

He surveyed the faces in the crowd of recruits, and others who were present. He began to speak, slowly and very distinctly.

"Good morning, men. I'm glad to see so many young men present, and I thank you for your patriotism. I know many of you have backgrounds as lumbermen and hunters and have been used to a hardy way of life. This lifestyle will be of great value to you in the days to come, as you will meet an enemy equally determined in their cause…an enemy, most of whom, have grown up with firearms and horses and are familiar with an outdoor way of life. I know most of you are well trained with rifles and shotguns and are good marksmen. That will be to our advantage. We have a hard task ahead of us, and it may be a long one, but we can face it with the confidence that the nation is behind us. Although we have no marching orders from the governor, you can expect to depart for Harrisburg on April twenty-fourth. My officers will have more information on that in the morning. In the meantime, if you have any questions or problems, see one of the officers. Good luck to us all, and thanks again for being here."

I clapped and cheered with the rest of the new men and said to my father and my friends, "I believe we have a fine commanding officer. He looks as though he means business and won't waste a lot of time in doing what needs to be accomplished."

"I'd follow him into battle without worrying too much," Cliff replied. Alex and Ed nodded in agreement.

"The only thing he said that bothered me a little was when he stated that our task might be a long one," Ed said.

I looked at Ed, saying, "Nobody can really tell for sure how long this war will last, and I suppose he didn't want to get our hopes up too high. If we have enough officers like him, it will be a big help in shortening the war, I think."

Father smiled and said, "I know you are going to be in good hands with this officer. Now, I've got to get going, so I'll say goodbye." He shook hands with each of the boys from Ceres and hugged me, saying, "By, remember what mother said, and don't take any unnecessary chances. Enjoyed being with you boys. You all write your folks soon as you can."

I walked over to my horse as father got up on the wagon and ran my fingers through his damp mane, rubbing his neck. "You be good, Buck," I said. "Take father home. Wait for me and I'll be home soon, too."

Father did not depart with an empty wagon. He took several of the extra items the men had brought with them from home and were told they wouldn't need, such as extra clothes. One of the officers told us we'd have to carry everything on our backs. We quickly decided the lighter, the better. Four horses belonging to the other recruits from the Ceres area were tied in trail behind the wagon.

We all waved and I stood a long time watching father drive out of sight. I wondered anew about my reasons for enlisting. I was glad to have reached the decision to do so, but I knew it could be many weeks or even months before I'd see my family again. What would happen to me in the meantime? I wiped away a few tears that had filled my eyes and thought it's never good to try to look too far ahead. If the others could handle it, I knew I could.

The next morning at muster I was surprised to learn that we would receive physical examinations. Col. Kane had enlisted the aid of several doctors to volunteer their services in determining if all the recruits were fit for service. I joked with one of the doctors. "I figured if we could walk in here under our own power, we would be acceptable. I never have seen so much interest in teeth. Why is that?"

Drifting To Glory

The doctor smiled and replied, "In addition to checking for diseased gums and bad teeth, we have to make sure you have at least two teeth that meet, top and bottom. That's not just so you can chew your food, but primarily it makes it possible for you to tear open the standard paper cartridges that the army uses. It enables you to pour the powder down the barrel of a muzzle loader, and eliminates the use of a powder horn. If you don't have at least two teeth that meet, you're disqualified."

"Well, I'll be damned," I exclaimed. "I hadn't thought about that."

Those men who were rejected by the physicians were very disappointed and quietly slipped out of camp. We watched them leave and felt sorry for them. I said, "Perhaps those poor guys are the lucky ones. Who knows?" We looked at one another and wondered.

We had some spare time in the afternoon. I suggested we walk down the street to see what Smethport had to offer. As we approached a butcher shop, we noticed a deer carcass hanging by the door. One of the recruits asked the butcher if he could have the tail, and the butcher was glad to give it to him. The recruit promptly pinned it to the side of his cap. As we walked back to camp, I laughed, saying, "I guess you have picked out a good insignia for the regiment."

He smiled and said, "I think this will be as good a badge as any to identify us by. Besides that, with as many deer as there are in the woods, we'll always have a good source for insignias." We all laughed at his logic.

Col. Kane noticed the man's cap as he walked up, and heartily approved of it, saying, "Hereafter, our regiment will be known as the 'Bucktails'."

By this time enough recruits were on hand to be organized into two companies, and depending upon where the men were from, we were called the McKean County Rifles and the Elk County Rifles. My friends and I were included in the McKean County Rifles.

Col. Kane administered the oath of allegiance, and we formed ranks, marching out of Smethport on April 24, 1861.

"I'm glad we're finally on our way," I said.

"Yeah, sitting around on our backsides, waiting for orders, can get pretty tiresome," Ed added.

The weather was fair, and we swung along at an easy pace, enjoying the scenery. Most of the road was through the woods, and we could feel the cool dampness of the foliage. The smell of the honeysuckle was almost overpowering. It was very pleasant. We made frequent stops where we quenched our thirst at cool streams or springs and filled our canteens.

Our enthusiasm had ebbed somewhat as we struggled wearily into Cameron Station, a march of almost twenty-seven miles! Few of us had ever walked that far in one day, especially with the weight of our packs. I noticed some of the men had discarded spare shoes or a blanket along the way.

"Well, Ed," I said, "I don't know about you, but I'm quite ready for some of that 'sitting around on our backsides' that you were talking about earlier!"

"You bet," Cliff added. "Thank goodness it's not really hot, yet. It really would be a tough hike lugging our gear on our backs and sweating all the way."

The Cameron County Rifles were waiting for us, and with those additional men, we now had sufficient numbers for three companies.

Everyone enjoyed a good evening meal, prepared in part by the good people of Cameron Station. They had prepared food for several days for the men who had already assembled there. We appreciated their efforts, knowing that it put a strain on the people and resources of the little village, but they seemed proud to extend any help that they could.

We gratefully turned in early after our first full day of hard marching. I had no problem dropping off to sleep.

Starting early on the twenty-fifth, we marched an additional fifteen miles to Driftwood, Pa., and Sinnemahoning Creek. A halt was ordered, and a meeting of the officers and men was held by the colonel. Rather than continue the overland march to Harrisburg, the idea was proposed to build rafts, and drift down the waterways to our destination of Harrisburg, Pa.

Many of the men, being familiar with the hilly terrain over which we must continue to march, listened intently as Col. Kane explained the situation. He asked if there were any questions or comments we wished to make.

I spoke up in response. "Yes sir. Could you tell us how many miles it is to Harrisburg from here, and wouldn't we lose a lot of time while we build rafts?"

The colonel answered, "I know we are all anxious to get to the capital, but we will have another 150 miles on foot. I believe it would take at least two days to build our rafts, and another three days, perhaps, to drift down the rivers. All things considered, I think we can at least equal our time on foot, and probably beat it. We would have several advantages in rafting. The creeks and rivers are high at this time of the year, and even if we get a lot of rain, we can make the same pace afloat. We'd surely move slower by marching on muddy roads. And remember this – we have many good woodsmen with us. We have the manpower to do the job. I'm sure the local folks will be pleased to loan us saws and axes and will help in any way they can."

The rafting proposal was put to a vote. It passed almost unanimously, with a few men against it who could not swim.

My friends and I were ready for a break in the marching. It had been pretty warm and often soggy along the country roads. We liked the idea of stretching out on a raft and letting the current do the work. I smiled as I painted a mental picture of the scene. "I always wanted to take a nice boat trip somewhere," I said. "Be fun to loll about and rest."

"Just as long as we don't have to get out and push," Ed chuckled. "It might not be as pleasurable as we think."

As Col. Kane had estimated, it did take two full days to build the rafts. Everyone pitched in and it made the job easier. We built four large rafts since almost three hundred men had to be transported. A rudder was placed at the rear of each raft. Long poles were cut from small saplings to be used to swing the rafts around shallow areas. We knew there would be some rocky spots where the poles would help, too.

One raft was made larger than the others. It was over sixty feet long, and almost twenty feet wide and would serve as the "headquarters" or command raft. Most of the men who would be officers boarded this raft, along with Col. Kane's horse. A small shanty or cabin was included for the colonel.

We thanked the townspeople who had been such a great help and pushed off, departing the Sinnemahoning area on April twenty-eighth. The creek was not much wider than our rafts in some places, and the poles came into use right away. We pushed the rafts away from the shores and the tangle of bushes and reeds that impeded our progress.

We discovered at once that all our loose personal gear had to be secured with ropes to keep the baggage from sliding overboard as we bobbed along in the current. We had wrapped our rifles in gunny sacks to protect them from the mud and water. Small lines were used to tie them to wooden cleats on the raft decks.

Soon after launching our small fleet into Sinnemahoning Creek, we encountered our first difficulties. The stream was swollen from spring rains and melting snow. The rafts drifted into the banks with the current, in spite of the rudder men doing their best to stay in mid stream. We repeatedly ran into bushes, reeds, and fallen trees where the high water had increased the width of the creek and overflowed the banks. At shallow depths, we took turns sliding into the cold water and helped to push and lift the rafts around obstructions.

I slipped in over my head at one point and came up spitting water and swearing. "Damn it, what happened to this business of lolling about and letting the current do the work?" Cliff and Ed were being helped back onto our raft by Alex and had to laugh at my plight. I was unable to keep from laughing at myself since we all shared the cold water dunking quite frequently that first day.

The current varied from five or six miles per hour to close to twice that speed as the creek twisted through narrow gorges and rocky sections in the rolling countryside. We continued to take turns in the shallow areas where we joined, shoulder to shoulder, to boost the rafts over the sandbars and rocks. It was tedious work.

Fortunately, conditions gradually improved. The farther we drifted, the wider the creek became, and when we entered the west branch of the Susquehanna River near Lock Haven, Pa., the river was much wider. We figured we wouldn't need to use the poles very often from this point to our destination, except in easing to shore and pushing off.

Our flotilla stopped for the night not far from Lock Haven. We drifted and poled the rafts into a serene little cove where spring was all around us. Crocus were in bloom and the trees were adorned with a new green growth of leaves.

As soon as we had secured the rafts, we began to collect wood for camp fires. No rain had fallen, so it was easy to start fires and prepare our first meal "at sea." Also, we had the chance to bathe in the river and wash our clothes.

Col. Kane and the officers from each company checked to determine if there had been any injuries among the men. None of us had been hurt, except for a few bruises. The men who were not swimmers had performed well on the rafts, using the poles and rudders to good advantage. The

Drifting To Glory

colonel was pleased that the day had gone so well and told us so.

Everyone was tired and very few had any dry clothes, so we hung most of our duds on sticks near the fires while we ate and wore the few dry clothes we could find. This proved to be a mite embarrassing, as it was not long until a group of well wishers, both men and women, arrived from town. Several officers quickly saved the day by meeting the visitors at the edge of the camp while some men covered themselves with blankets, and the rest of us scampered into our tents for cover. The townsfolk welcomed those of our number who did come out to say hello. They stated that our passage had been noted along the streams and that the flag and bucktails had been seen flying over the rafts. They said we could probably expect more greeters all along our route to Harrisburg since we would be drifting into areas of heavier population, especially as the river valley widened.

The colonel kept the visits as short as he could, advising the folks that the men had to turn in soon, explaining that they had spent a hard first day. Also, he stated that we needed to rise early to get a good start in the morning. He thanked them for their interest and the courtesy of the visits.

The people who had come by the camp had been so friendly that I thought maybe a little visit to town might be fun. We were all tired, but I figured a little diversion might be good for us. I discussed the idea with Cliff and Alex. Ed had not felt too well and decided to turn in early.

"I'll go for it," Cliff said. "We need to relax and enjoy ourselves a bit...can't be more than a mile to town."

"Count me in, too," Alex piped up.

"Since no one had said anything about the town being out of bounds, I don't see how we can get into much difficulty," I said as we slipped quietly out of camp.

We sauntered down the road in the pleasant coolness of the evening. The church spires of town appeared quickly, and we turned the corner and walked into the main street. Almost immediately we were noticed by one of the men who had been at our camp earlier in the evening. He came over to us, saying, "Hello, fellas. What brings you to town? It doesn't matter, 'cause we're glad to see you young men for any reason. We're mighty proud of what you are doing for your country. Some of the local lads will be joining up very shortly. I just wish I was young enough to go, too. The least I can do is to buy you a drink."

He led us across the dusty street to a quaint old tavern with ivy creeping up the walls. The walls were hewn out of logs, and a stone chimney stood at each end. Smoke spiraled from one chimney.

Our new friend ordered some wine for us. He introduced us to his friends, and we soon learned that several of them were Mexican War veterans. In a minute we were all sitting at a large table, and the proprietor appeared with trays of sandwiches which he said were his contribution to the war effort for the evening for such distinguished guests as ourselves. Free drinks kept appearing on the table...more than we needed, but we didn't want to refuse the hospitality.

The old veterans told us about their Mexican War experiences. They said they knew the army would supply us with weapons and equipment far better than they had used. With any kind of good leadership they figured, like everyone else, that we'd be home before the end of the year. One of them remarked, "Hell, I read the other day that there isn't even a cannon factory in the whole south! Once the Rebels run out of the goods to fight with, it'll be all over but the shouting, even if they have good men to fight with."

We enjoyed their war stories and recounted our rafting experiences thus far. Our account became a little on the exaggerated side, taking into consideration the drinks we had consumed. I said, "If we don't get lost or sink, I think we'll finally get to the war before it ends."

Cliff looked at the big old clock on the wall over the bar and asked, "By, you think maybe we better be heading back to camp?"

It was after midnight. The old guy chewing on a cigar stub who had been playing a decrepit piano in the corner, closed the lid on the old upright. He said, "I'm all played out. Time for me to call it a night and head for the house." He came over to our table, wished us good luck and left the tavern. Without his playing, the tavern became much more like a study room. Everyone had left but our little group.

One of the old soldiers said, "Oh the night is still young, but if you young fellers is worried about the walk back to camp, stand at ease. We'll hustle you back over there in a jiffy in my wagon."

The stories and jokes continued for a few more minutes, and I finally said, "We'll take you up on that ride back to camp. In our present condition it could be a long staggering trip. We might not make it before sunup." We all laughed at what I had said.

Alex chuckled and started to get up from his chair, lost his footing, and fell down. This brought on more giggling as we got Alex to his feet and started to the wagon.

As we left the tavern, I thanked the proprietor for his kindness, and we stepped out into the still night. Stars were shining in a cloudless sky, and a near full moon cast long shadows in the town. The cool air felt soothing to us and helped to clear our heads a little.

The old vet slowly headed his wagon in the direction of the camp and reassured us we'd be there in no time. I told the driver and his pal that we hadn't informed anyone that we were going to town and didn't want to disturb anyone on the way back into camp. "In fact," I said, "I think it would be best if you drop us off out here about a quarter mile short of camp. We can walk in quietly without the sound of a horse and wagon and hope that we haven't been missed."

Our good friends agreed. We thanked them for all their hospitality and shook hands all around. They wished us the best of luck and turned the wagon back toward town, singing softly as they went.

Alex had been snoozing on the way out of town, but he started talking as we started walking. He said, "Yes sir, we'd better get back in quietly before we're accused of desertion...hate to be kicked out 'fore we're hardly signed in."

I looked at Cliff and Alex. "Wouldn't it be a joke if something had happened to us in town, and we had missed the raft?" I said. "We probably would be absent for the desertion court martial, too!" We all snickered at the thought, and to make it worse, we heard the old vets increase the volume of their singing in the distance. That caused a little more laughter.

Cliff said, "This is like being in church and getting tickled when you know you're not supposed to be laughing."

"The Three Musketeers," as we had decided to call ourselves, stumbled down the path away from the main entrance to the camp. We didn't want to alert the sentry who had been posted there. It was almost two o'clock. The camp fires had died out and it was very quiet. We made our way as cautiously as possible over to our tent area. Cliff stumbled over a tent stake and fell down, got up, and fell over a tent rope. "Damn it anyhow," he said in hushed tones. Unbeknown to us, Col. Kane was standing outside his tent smoking a cigar in the still of the night. His tent was not far from where ours were located, and he noticed the disturbance. He didn't speak, but evidently made a mental note of it and turned in.

Reveille came much to early, and the sound of the bugle grated on the nerves of those who had turned in late. It was not a welcome noise. The camp came to life as pots and pans rattled in the preparation of breakfast. With no wind, the area quickly became covered with a blanket of smoke from the breakfast fires.

Ed dressed quickly and said, "Boy, I slept like a log, especially after all that hard work yesterday. You guys don't look all that bright eyed this morning. Didn't you sleep well?" He couldn't restrain a smile since he had heard us come in during the night and couldn't help rubbing it in a little, especially since he hadn't gone with us.

"Ah, the ground in our tent was rough, and it was hard to get comfortable," Cliff said.

Ed shot back, "Sure it was, and I'll bet that road back from town was rough and uncomfortable, too!"

We looked at one another and laughed, in spite of how badly we felt after too much to drink and only four hours sleep.

Ed added, "You midnight rovers have got to be more careful if you're going to burn the midnight oil, especially if you've been to visit old 'John Barleycorn' at a tavern somewhere. Alex smelled like a brewery when he crawled into the tent last night, or should I say just a while ago?"

Breakfast completed, Col. Kane called us together to outline the progress he expected us to make for the day. He said, "Since the river will be wider and deeper now, I believe we'll have no trouble making it to Williamsport, Pa. There is the possibility that we might have rail cars waiting for us there. I telegraphed the governor before we left Smethport, and he indicated they would do all possible to have some rail transportation available. He did caution me that all rail rolling stock is in short supply.

The colonel then added some additional remarks before we loaded and boarded the rafts.

"It came to my attention that we have a few nomads among us who wandered off into the dark last night. While I did not specifically restrict you men to camp, I assumed everyone would be so tired from yesterday's exertions that you would all be ready to turn in early. Evidently, this was not the case. I want to inform you now, however, that I do not expect a repeat performance by any other midnight drifters! You men are to confine your drifting to the rafts until we arrive at Harrisburg. Is that understood by everyone?"

Drifting To Glory

A resounding "Yes, sir!" echoed throughout the camp. Those of us who were included within the midnight drifters looked at each other and smiled broadly.

The colonel could not help smiling as he turned away, and began to chat with some of his officers. He knew what we had done was actually good for morale and would give the other men something to talk about for several days.

As we returned to begin loading our gear, we laughed about our deed and the colonel's comments. I said, "Guess we got away with it this time, but we'd be wise to toe the line in the future, I think." Everyone agreed.

We all broke camp, finished loading our equipment on the rafts, and shoved off again at about eight o'clock, April twenty-ninth. What the colonel had said about the condition of the river was correct. The Susquehanna was now wider and deeper. Rafting now became a pleasure with the rudder men taking turns to keep the rafts in mid stream. We were able to rest and loll about on the rafts as I had suggested earlier. Some men played cards or talked about what would happen when we got to Harrisburg. Others just sat and watched the scenery go·by, occasionally waving to people on the shore.

The "night wanderers," as we had been named were able to get a few hours of much needed sleep. Fair weather clouds were drifting across the river when we awoke, and a bright sun added to the beautiful day. There was just enough breeze to put a ripple on the otherwise calm water. Most of the men removed their shirts to enjoy the sunshine and breeze.

We ate the leftover biscuits and dried beef from last night's meal. One of the recruits began to play a harmonica, and we all sang or hummed along. It was more like a river cruise in peaceful times than a voyage from which many of us might not return. I didn't want to think about thoughts like that in such a festive setting and blanked them out of my mind.

By mid afternoon, our rafts were at Williamsport, and we poled them to the shore very close to town. Camp was set up as on the previous day. We were getting faster at making camp. The mayor and town officials stopped by for a visit. They welcomed us and the mayor sat down to talk with the colonel.

The mayor said, "I'm afraid I'm the bearer of some discouraging news for you and your troops. I have a wire from the governor, and it outlines that the state can only accept a maximum of two companies from your area, or only about half the number you have with you. We have received rail cars for about one hundred-fifty men. You see, there is a shortage of cars because more men have been signing up than anticipated."

Col. Kane thanked the mayor for the information, told him he would discuss it at once, and would decide how to proceed in the morning.

The colonel assembled the men and explained the dilemma. We were all disappointed, and no one wanted to turn around and go home. We told our commander that we would continue to Harrisburg, one way or another, come what may. We were determined. The colonel replied, "I can certainly understand the way you feel, and I am in complete agreement with you. We will continue tomorrow, if not by rail, then on our rafts again."

"Three cheers for the colonel," someone shouted, and we all joined in. We knew our colonel would not let us down.

We watched as the colonel left camp in the morning and rode to town to confer with the mayor. The officers directed us to tidy up the camp in preparation for departing.

When the colonel returned, he discussed the results of the visit with his officers. The officers passed the word to the individual companies. We listened as our captain spoke to us. "Men, true to his word, the colonel has told the mayor that we are going to continue on the rail cars provided for us. The three cars on hand are not enough for us all to ride comfortably, so we're going to have to strap some equipment on the roofs. Some of you can also ride on top, and others will have to take turns sitting in the aisles and standing on the landings between cars. I think we can work it out without too much difficulty. In case you are wondering what we'll do with our rafts, the mayor is arranging to pay us for them. That will give us a little money to set up some company funds that will come in handy later. The mayor said Williamsport can use the rafts to supplement the old rafts and barges they have been using."

We busied ourselves over the next few hours transferring our equipment from the camp to the rail cars. One of the cars was a box car, and we loaded most of the equipment in this car, with space provided for the colonel's horse.

The afternoon was almost gone before we finished loading. We were advised not to load the tents. The colonel thought it would be wise to spend the night and start in the morning. He explained that we could arrive in Harrisburg earlier in the day, and he would have more time to discuss the acceptance of the entire number of men with the governor. He doubted anyone would be sent home.

The good people of Williamsport had prepared food to take on the train, and when it was learned that we would remain until morning, the food was used to make an evening meal for us. The ladies baked pies and cakes for desert in addition to what was already prepared. We made a point of complimenting them on providing such a sumptuous meal on such short notice.

After the meal, tables were moved in the town square where we had eaten, and the area became a big dance floor. A banjo player, fiddler, and a guitar player appeared, and several of the recruits joined them with their instruments to make a good band for us. Everyone joined the singing and dancing.

Alex said, "Maybe these delays in getting to the capital are not so bad after all." We smiled with him as he complimented a pretty lass who he'd been dancing with.

"We'll have to be sure you show up for muster in the morning, Al," I said. "We can't have you deserting before we even get to the war."

Alex's friend and the girls we had met agreed that they would be happy for us to remain longer, but knew that we couldn't.

As I sat tapping my feet to the music, I said, "We're having a grand old time for being in a war." When I said it, I was aware that these good times wouldn't last, and that all was not right. A foreboding of future events came over me as I watched the dancers, not really seeing them, as I thought:

I wish I could turn the page in this period of my life and see what will happen in the weeks ahead. Maybe I'd feel better about the whole business. On the other hand, a view of the future might not be such a good idea. It might scare me half to death if I could see what's going to happen to me. Hell, I'll be smart to take it just one damn day at a time.

I pushed the thought out of my mind as I said, "How about whirling around this stone dance floor one more time before we call it a night?"

The hour became late and the folks started to return to their homes. We recruits lingered, however, and chatted with the young girls we had met. We asked for addresses and promised to write from Harrisburg and elsewhere when we could. My friend, Alex, made sure he had the address of the young woman he had met since he was quite fascinated with her.

On the morning of May first, the small train was made ready for departure. We stored the bulkier items on top of the cars and our haversacks of personal gear in the cars, making sure our names were attached.

The short train was ready to pull away at eight o'clock. We said goodbye to the young ladies and others who had come to see us off. We had tarried until the last minute, and when the whistle sounded and the train started moving, we had to hustle to make it on board. The urging of the officers helped, too. The Union flag and bucktails could be seen flying from a mast on the last car of our procession.

We were among the last few men to clamber on board, and thus had to take what was left of the spacious accommodations. We ended up sitting on the steps and landings between cars and were bombarded with cinders encased in coal smoke.

By mid day the train, pulled by what proved to be a wheezing, dilapidated, old engine, had made only fifty miles. We arrived at Sunbury, Pa. At this juncture in our odyssey, problems arose once more. The train was halted by order of the governor who restated his order that a maximum of two companies of men would be accepted at this time. We left the cars in an angry mood, but Col. Kane talked to the officers, and they assured us that the colonel would straighten out the problem with the governor in person. The train was ordered on to Harrisburg with just the colonel and a few officers.

Hurriedly unloading again, we set up tents on the edge of town in a light drizzle. The dark skies appeared to offer more than just a drizzle before morning.

I shook my head and said, "I have a feeling the colonel may have a tough time persuading the governor to take us all. I think they ought to take every man or none of us, but I'll bet the colonel has a tough row to hoe to convince the governor to do it!"

Chapter IV

May second dawned wet and gloomy. Our mood matched the weather. It had rained most of the night, and we had not pitched our tents in the best locations. Our bed rolls and most of our clothes were soaked, and it was difficult finding dry wood to start fires for breakfast. We were a bunch of wet chickens and were disgusted with the situation. We all realized we had things to learn about sleeping outdoors in weather conditions that could vary daily. I had bunked with Cliff in one small tent; Alex and Ed in a tent beside us. We called them "dog tents" because they were hardly large enough for a big dog to take shelter in, let alone two men. We each carried half a tent with us. We could button the halves together, draping them over an improvised ridgepole or stretch them between two trees. Both ends were open.

We moved our tents to higher ground where the drainage was better, just in case we had to remain in Sunbury for a few more days.

"It looks like the sun is going to hang around," I said. "Let's string up our wet stuff. Maybe we can get everything dried out before dark."

Cliff placed his hands on his hips and smiled at me, saying, "By, you're such a damned optimist. I bet you'll have corporal stripes on your sleeves before we fire the first shot!"

"I don't want any stripes," I answered. "I just want to get in, get the war over with, and get out all in one piece."

Cliff and my pals laughed. "I'm with you on that," Cliff said. "Now if you'll look over there on that slope, there's some trees we can string our clothes between. The breeze is picking up and should dry our things out pretty quick. See, I can be an optimistic cuss, too."

As the weather improved, so did our dispositions. All the men felt better about our situation.

Alex brought up the subject of the governor's limitation on our numbers. "Do you think the colonel can actually convince the governor to take all three companies?"

Ed responded defiantly, "Al, I sure as hell hope so, but if not, I have a good mind to pack up and go home, oath of allegiance or not. If they don't need us bad enough to take us all, well, I can think of a whole bunch of things I can be doing this spring and summer."

"Let's not kick over the traces, yet, fellas," I said, trying to sound as calm as possible. "We've come this far without too much trouble. I think we just need to be patient. I know how you feel, but the army is going to be suffering some growing pains getting everyone signed up and equipped. Chances are they're going to need us all before they get this war resolved. It would be a damned shame if any of us have to go home, but the colonel's a persuasive man, and you can count on him to fix things before we see him again."

Ed smiled and calmed down. "I know you're right, By," he said, "'course I'll hang around 'til we get the word, but I just hope we hear soon. This waiting is a pain in the ass."

Alex suggested, "While we're just sitting around waiting for our laundry to dry like a bunch of old women, why don't we get up a card game to help pass the time? Maybe it would be good to get our minds on something else."

Cliff chuckled. "Good thinking," he said. "With a little bit of luck, I might be able to increase my skinny bank roll. I'm almost broke, and God only knows when we'll get our first pay."

We played penny ante poker for an hour or so. Cliff laughed as he ended up the big winner with over four dollars. "Tell you what," he said. "With this stake when we get to Harrisburg, I'm buying dinner for all you poor losers." None of us objected.

Col. Kane returned on the afternoon of the third of May. We were all assembled as the colonel climbed up on a makeshift table to speak. "Well, boys, I have returned with good news for everyone. After considerable urging, Governor Curtin has agreed to accept all three companies at one time." We all waved our caps and cheered. The colonel smiled broadly and went on. "Thank goodness we didn't recruit more companies from our neck of the woods, or he would have turned me down! We will be mustered in as part of the Pennsylvania Reserve Volunteer Corps."

He continued, "I regret there will be another delay, but only a short one. Today is Friday, and we can't arrive at the capital until Sunday, the fifth, because they just can't do anything with us until Monday. I had the opportunity to inspect the facilities at Camp Curtin, and they are short of everything. Some barracks and mess halls are being constructed. Fortunately, we have our own tents. They are making arrangements for feeding everyone, but the uniforms are lacking, as well as the other accouterments we'll need. My advice is for you men to clean up the clothing you have and see that your rifles are clean, as well as any other gear you may have with you. We want to arrive looking as much like soldiers as possible. We'll plan on leaving Sunbury early Sunday morning. It's only a short run to Harrisburg…about forty miles or so. We'll have rail cars here Saturday.

"That is all I have to report to you, except for this suggestion. Since we have another full day before we depart, I urge you men to write a few lines to your families and tell them that you are well and being taken care of. I know your loved ones are anxious to hear from you, and a letter or postal card will do a lot to relieve their minds."

Having concluded his remarks, the colonel jumped off the table and returned to the officers' area. We stood around in little groups discussing his remarks. Everyone was pleased that the delays were over, and we'd finally be getting to our destination. We were in a jovial mood as we returned to our tent area.

Ed looked puzzled and said, "By the way, can someone please tell me just what the heck 'accouterments' are? I never heard the word until the colonel used it."

I said, "Don't feel like you're the only one who's not familiar with that word. I wouldn't have known what it meant either, except that I read it in Harper's Weekly about six weeks ago. They printed a list of military terms, and defined 'accouterments' as covering a soldier's equipment, other than his arms and uniforms."

Ed said, "Well, damn, I guess you can learn something every day if you go to the right place!"

"Yeah, but are you sure this is the right place?" Alex said, laughing.

Ed laughed, too, and was silent for a few seconds. Then he said with a serious look on his face, "Well, you fellas will have to excuse me. I've got to go check to see if all my accouterments are in order."

We all got a kick out of his joke and laughed about it as we stretched out in the soft grass next to our tents, waiting to see what had been rounded up for lunch.

Drifting To Glory

That evening and during the day on Friday, we cleaned up our equipment and washed some clothes in the river. We looked like a bunch of scrub women with soap, wash rags, and brushes. We washed ourselves, too, and killed two birds with one piece of soap.

Most of the men followed the colonel's suggestion and wrote letters to our folks. Some men were already a mite homesick, but were careful not to let it show in their letters. It seemed odd but I didn't miss home, at least not yet. I had never been away from home for more than a day or two. Thus far I was enjoying new things...the new towns and scenery, the comradeship of men in the same situation, and the prospect of a quick victory. I tried to keep these positive thoughts ever present.

On Saturday a locomotive backed five cars into Sunbury. We looked and laughed at what we saw. I said, "These are all old cattle cars. They must be getting ready to send us to the slaughter house!" Several men did not see the humor in what I had said. The cars had been cleaned out, and benches had been fixed across the width of the cars. At least we had two more cars than we had been furnished at Williamsport and would not be so crowded on this last short leg of our trip. Our loading was completed, except for the tents on Saturday afternoon.

That evening, as in Williamsport, the townspeople appeared with good food, and another band played for us. Most of the men wished that we had a longer journey to get to the capital. We were beginning to get used to all the attention we had received along our route. We bid the townfolk farewell late in the evening, thanking them for their thoughtfulness.

Early Sunday morning we pulled down our tents. We loaded them with our personal gear, and waved to those who had come to see us off. Our train headed down the tracks in a cloud of smoke with the engineer tooting the whistle to say good-bye. An enthusiastic mood prevailed among the men...Harrisburg at last!

Chapter V

Our train arrived at Camp Curtin at nine o'clock. We had been expected and a military band was on hand to greet us as we unloaded. Gen. George McCall, the commanding officer of the camp, welcomed us and his subordinates were on hand to show us to our camp quarters. We were told that this would be our home for the next few weeks.

The general explained to Col. Kane that the Bucktails were lucky to have been accepted. Other recruits had been turned back and returned home. Many men had to remain at home. They were told that they would be called as soon as the situated warranted.

The status at Camp Curtin was one of confusion. As Col. Kane had told us, there was a great lack of uniforms, rifles, ammunition, and all the accouterments that would be needed by a fledgling army. These things were scheduled to be coming down the government pipeline. To make matters worse, it had not rained for some time and dust covered everything. The many regular troops we saw looked like Confederates due to the heavy gray coating of dust on their uniforms.

The disorderly state of affairs did not prevent some progress from being made. Gen. McCall issued an order for us to formally elect our officers, and the companies were given letter designations. The Bucktail regiment became the 13th Pa. Reserves, also known as our volunteer number, the 42nd Pa. Reserves. The McKean County Rifles became Company "I." I was included in this company with my friends.

Our company commander was Capt. Blanchard. Col. Kane, although originally elected as colonel of the regiment, decided to step down in favor of Col. Biddle who had been in the Mexican War and had considerable military experience. Col. Kane was pleased to serve as Lt. Col. of the regiment.

One of the first changes that we Bucktails were made aware of was the fact that the state allotment for the total number of men to be enlisted had been reached. Instead of enlisting for three months as originally agreed to, we would have to sign for three years! Everyone agreed to this as we all believed the war had little chance of lasting one year, let alone three.

Our regiment settled down to routine duties. Guard duty was usually an unpleasant task, but latrine duty was worse. Each man took his turn at both assignments. Gradually the uniforms arrived. Being issued a uniform that was a good fit was unusual. We were anxious to try them on. It was a joke. I got pants that were too big in the waist, and Cliff got pants that were the right length but too small in the waist. We swapped trousers and were satisfied with the fit. Swapping worked better than trying to get the quartermaster's people to make changes. The same thing happened with the shoes. We were advised to take a size that was slightly too large because our feet would swell after much marching, and small shoes would cause blisters. Also, wet shoes would shrink when they dried and cause the same problems. Most of us found a kepi that fit our heads.

After our noon meal on the day we were issued our new uniforms, the word was passed for us to assemble by companies in our mess hall. Mess halls had been erected with a roof and both ends enclosed with the sides left open. At one end the food was prepared, and at the other end the area contained the tin plates and cups, eating utensils, and deep sinks for washing. The idea of leaving the sides of the mess halls open was twofold. It helped to expedite the construction of so many mess halls for the thousands of recruits, and with the summer weather coming, it would be cooler for the men. As colder weather arrived, the sides of the buildings could be completed and coal stoves installed. I figured someone had done a lot of planning on short notice.

Company "I" remained in the mess area after the noon meal was finished. One of our officers appeared and told us that a sergeant would be along in a few minutes to give us the details of our training. The lieutenant had just left the building when a soldier in regular army uniform appeared. He walked to the end of the hall and hopped up on one of the tables so we could all see him. Conversation tapered off among the men so we could hear him. We wondered about the information we were about to receive. Everyone eyed the sergeant from heat to foot. He was almost six feet tall and had a stocky build. I whispered to Cliff that he looked as though he could hold his own in a saloon brawl. The sergeant had bright blue eyes that had a twinkle to them as if he knew things, good and bad, that he could relate to us from years of experience.

He looked slowly around the company of men as if to size us up, put his hands on his hips, and began to speak in a loud voice. "Sergeant Ray McNew is my name and training is my new game!" Everyone grinned and listened as he went on. "I have been given the dubious honor of training companies "H" and "I" in the finer arts of drilling, shooting, and all the other activities involved in soldiering. This war came on us in a hurry and we are short of men who know how to train new recruits, but you greenhorns are in luck having a seasoned old cuss like me to guide you. I'm told that I have only six weeks or so to whip you into shape, so you ladies are going to have to cooperate, buckle down, and work hard." More smiles and laughter rippled through the crowd. The sergeant smiled, too, and droned on. "I have been in this old army for seventeen years, served as a lad in the war with Mexico, and fought in the second Seminole Indian War in the fifties. I've learned some things that I think will help to keep you youngsters alive. All I ask is that you listen to me, keep your noses clean, and do as you're told. If you do that, you'll get along fine, and 'Uncle Abraham,' and I will be very proud of you. We'll begin in the morning right after you have another fine army breakfast. Do you have any questions? Try to make them short and easy to answer. My time is very valuable." He smiled again and pointed at Alex who had raised his hand.

"Sergeant, do you think this war will be over so that we can all be home by Christmas?" A few men laughed, but they hoped we would be home and were glad Alex asked the question.

Sgt. McNew paused before answering. "I have heard what you men have…that this will be a short war lasting six months at the most. As I've told you, I have fought in Mexico and did so along side of officers and men who were from the south. They were good men in the U.S. Army, and I'm sure those who went south will do well in the Confederate Army. Many fine officers will be leading them. Those men are as determined in their cause and love their land as you do yours. I believe we will come out on top in this war, but I'd be afraid to say how long it will take us to win it. Let me put it this way. I wouldn't count on being home for Christmas this year and have my doubts about next year. Now, that's just my opinion. We'll talk again."

After that statement, most other questions were forgotten. We looked at one another and began to chat. We were all a little discouraged. I said, "I wonder if we made a mistake signing for three years?"

Ed said, "Naw, I think the government just has to protect itself, and make sure they'll have enough troops on hand."

As we walked back to our tent area, Cliff added, "You know, the population up here is much greater than down south. We should be able to field an army much larger than the Rebs can come up with. If we all do our part, it ought to keep this war from going on too many months. At least we can hope so. Damned if I want to make a career of the army!"

The recruit training began in earnest the next morning. I listened with the other men as Sgt. McNew explained the basic rudiments of the various commands. We would learn to march at first without our rifles which we learned to stack by our tents. The sergeant enlisted the aid of a few regular army privates to show us how to follow the commands. Most of us had no experience in drilling, and our instructors could not restrain their laughter as some men turned left, instead of right when the order "column right" was given. Recruits ran into one another as we turned the wrong direction; a few tripped and fell down. It was all very amusing to us, too, and anyone else who happened to be passing the drill field.

Sgt. McNew exclaimed, "Damn, it's a good thing we don't have you carrying your rifles, yet. Someone could be hit in the head and laid out as a casualty before we're in combat."

In order to make it easier for the recruits to follow the marching instructions, Sgt. McNew tried an old routine. He knew the country lads knew the difference between hay and straw. He had them tie some hay to one shoe and straw to the other shoe. Instead of ordering "left" and "right" he'd shout "hayfoot" – "strawfoot," and the boys caught on to that pretty fast. The drill would sound like this: "left, right – hayfoot, strawfoot – left, right." It didn't take long to discard the hay and straw. Those of us who watched the drill had to admit the simple things work best.

Our days quickly stretched into weeks, and we became very proficient at drilling, with and without rifles. After a particularly long, hot day of drilling, I said, "I think I know why they are drilling us into the ground with this damned marching. I'm convinced they're doing it to conserve ammunition. Some fat general had a bright idea. They expect us to dazzle the enemy to death with our fancy footwork!"

Cliff laughed and said, "Yeah, the Rebs will be so hypnotized that we can march right through their lines and take them all prisoner without firing a shot!"

Alex and Ed looked at each other, and Alex said, "I think you two guys are beginning to show the first signs of sunstroke, or the dust may have coated your brains. The true reason we are doing all this marching is to break in these stiff new shoes. Also, I think old sarge McNew hasn't drilled any troops recently, and he wants to make himself look good in front of the officers. He's determined to be the last man standing after we all fall on our faces from exhaustion. He'll make sergeant major soon."

The next day we were at it again. It was very hot and humid, and big swelling clouds drifted across the campsite. We hoped for rain, but there was no relief. Sgt. McNew was aware of how tired we were and ordered a halt in the drilling. We were given a break after another final period of drill. The sergeant walked back to a shady area where the non-commissioned officers hung out. We picked a shady area in a small grove of trees and proceeded to stack our rifles. I was a little careless and when I attached my rifle to the neat pyramid of other arms, I knocked the whole stack over. One of the rifles belonged to Pvt. Dawley, one of the biggest men in our company.

It was only a few seconds until I heard a voice say, "Hey, Danforth, what the hell are you doing? Can't you stack a rifle like anyone else?" Several of the men thought it was funny, but Dawley didn't. He said, "I take good care of my rifle, polish the stock, and protect it from scratches. You better hope it's not beat up or you're liable to be!" he added sarcastically.

The heat and the drilling had worn me out, and my temper was on the short side. I snapped back at him, saying, "Listen, buddy, I'm sorry if I've put a scratch on your damned piece. Why don't you just take that rifle and shove it up your ass, and that way you'll always have it protected!"

Cliff grabbed my arm. "I'm afraid you've done it now, By," he said. "Why don't you laugh and make light of it. If you tell him you're sorry, he'll forget about it."

"Hell no, I won't," I answered. "I meant what I said." I realized I had probably made a mistake as soon as I spoke.

Dawley got to his feet quickly for a big man, and a circle of men quickly formed around us as he came over to me and said, "I'm going to show you who needs protection, you little peckerwood. No son of a bitch speaks to me like that." He grabbed my right shoulder with his left hand and hit me square on the jaw with a big right fist. I dropped like a sack of potatoes. My jaw hurt and I thought I was going to pass out. I saw Dawley straddling me acting like he was going to jump on me. I knew I couldn't wrestle the big oaf. I shook my head and struggled back on my feet. He tried to hit me again, but he was too slow, and I sidestepped his blow to the right and caught him with my right as hard as I could on his nose. I felt his nose break and blood trickled down his lip. Now I was afraid I had really made him mad and protected myself as much as I could as he missed me, punching at my body. I hit him with my left to his mid section which didn't seem to bother him at all. He dropped his guard, trying to ward off the punch, and when he did, I punched at his face with my right. He moved his head backward and my fist hit him in the throat. The fight was over. Dawley crumpled to the ground holding his throat, making a gurgling sound. I knew from school yard brawls that there is nothing more painful than to be hit in the throat with a hard blow.

Sgt. McNew and an officer arrived to see the end of the struggle. Lieutenant Rice directed two men to help Dawley to the medical department. The lieutenant looked at me and said, "I heard the shouting and saw the fracas from the distance, and I know the big guy threw the first punch. I'm surprised you escaped without a broken neck, Danforth, and that you didn't end up in the hospital. I'm going to talk with Dawley and tell him just what I'm telling you now. There will be no more fighting among the men in this regiment, except for scheduled boxing matches. If I find out that you have been mixing it up again, you'll find yourself on guard duty for a month, and you can kiss good-bye any leave to go home when we get that opportunity. You save your fighting for the Rebs where it will do us all some good. Do I make myself clear, soldier?"

"Yes sir, lieutenant," I answered. "I doubt I'd live through a repeat performance with that giant, anyhow, sir." Lt. Rice smiled as I saluted and walked away shaking his head. I returned to our area with a very sore jaw and a headache. My buddies started calling me "champ," but I discouraged that.

We finally got the chance to shoot our rifles and demonstrate our marksmanship. Unfortunately, a turn of events came about that disappointed everyone. We had brought our own personal rifles with us, but they were of such a variety of weapons and calibers that it would have created a huge problem to supply the different ammunition and parts needed. The officers told us the army was trying to standardize the small arms, but newer guns wouldn't be on hand in quantity for some months. We would be issued older flintlock muskets, which had been modified for more modern use. We would have to use the older guns until the army could supply us with the standard Springfield or Enfield rifles. We were not happy about that.

By the end of June, we were supplied with the equipment required to take to the field as a fighting unit. We were issued new haversacks to carry the smaller items on our backs. Ed laughed about the quantity of items, saying, "I'm glad we have finally been issued all our accoutrements. I'd hate to think we might go off campaigning without each and every piece they think we need."

I laughed at him and said, "Now if we can just carry all this stuff and fight too, we may do all right."

We received our first regular pay after a month in the army, and were allowed passes into Harrisburg. Thirteen dollars seemed like a lot compared to the little change we had left since enlisting. Some of the men owed it all to the men they had been gambling with over the past weeks.

The camp commander allowed only a few companies to visit Harrisburg at one time, rather than turning us all loose like a stampede of cattle on the town's resources. It was very pleasant to see something other than the same old dusty camp areas. The flowers, nice green yards, and fountains in the downtown area were refreshing to view. We enjoyed seeing the capitol buildings and grounds, which none of us had ever seen.

One thing we had longed for was a good meal in a nice restaurant. After the steak dinner, which we reminded Cliff that he owed us from his poker winnings, we sought out other forms of entertainment. We put in an appearance at the fancy saloon adjoining the restaurant; however, on this occasion we restrained ourselves and did not over indulge in what was available. We knew we would be required to muster early the next morning.

In the evening, we somehow found ourselves in a less reputable section of the city. Here a number of us satisfied another longing we had been denied over the past few weeks. It was a very busy establishment, and we noticed a lack of any patrols from the provost marshal's department. Evidently, we were being allowed some leeway as new soldiers. A number of young lads lost their innocence and their two dollars in a hurry, but everyone agreed it was money well spent.

On the way back to camp, we noticed with interest the expansion activities at one of the hospitals on the edge of the city. A sign indicated that the expansion was a result of efforts made by the U.S. Sanitary Commission in anticipation of the increase in military casualties expected in the weeks ahead. We hoped we would be spared the opportunity of seeing the facilities from the inside. The sign was removed after several high ranking officers complained that it was demoralizing. No one had to be reminded that casualties would increase.

Chapter VI

Our training was completed in late June, and the men of the training command, including Sgt. McNew, wished the regiment well. In a few days, the Bucktails were ordered into the northwestern part of the Virginia-Maryland area. The people living in the mountainous sections of this region were mainly loyal to the Union and welcomed our presence.

Several companies of our regiment, including Co. "I" marched across a narrow section of Maryland near Cumberland and the area of Virginia near Keyser and Romney. Here our company saw its first action and caused our first enemy casualties with no losses to ourselves.

Co. "I" had been deployed forward as skirmishers along the edge of a wooded area. I was lying in a thicket with Cliff to my right. We could see Alex and Ed to our left. As we were lying there quietly, Rebel infantrymen appeared approximately fifty yards ahead of us in a slight clearing. It was hot and I could see the sweat on the faces of the men as they advanced. I could even make out the Enfield rifles they carried.

"I don't think they've seen us, Cliff," I whispered. "Get ready to fire." We were all afraid, and I had to keep wiping the sweat out of my eyes.

My God, I thought. This is it. I wish they would turn around and go back, and I wish I were someplace else!

The Rebels came slowly forward and spotted us. Dropping to the ground they shot at us. Little puffs of dirt sprang up, and I could actually hear the minie balls whistle past me. As long as they just keep going by me, I thought, that's fine. I watched as a Reb rose up on one knee to fire, and I took careful aim and fired. I heard him groan as he fell over. The rest of the platoon was firing, and I saw another man fall when Cliff fired. The Rebel troops retreated to seek better cover, and the order was passed to the Bucktails to fall back.

It had been a small, quick skirmish. As we discussed it that evening, I said, "You know, I had a choice the first time I fired. I could have shot a man about my own age, but I picked out an older, bearded guy. I reasoned he was the more experienced of the two, and I wouldn't have to face him again. It made sense to me. I guess I've killed for the first time, and I'm not especially proud of it. How do you guys feel about it?"

Cliff could see I was nervous as I spoke about it. He said, "It's not really pleasant to shoot a man, but the fact is, that's why we're here. If you hadn't shot the man, he probably would have shot you or one of us. So, there you are. It's like I said about killing deer. It won't be so hard the next time. It's sad but true."

Alex and Ed said they had fired several shots, but were not positive that they had hit anyone. It's not always easy to tell when so much is happening.

While not scouting the area and performing picket duty, our training continued. We learned more about executing the standard military movements, especially with regard to wheeling lines of men into position for action from different types of terrain.

By late July, our regiment had received the news of the Union defeat at the battle of Bull run. The reserve regiments were all ordered to return to the Harrisburg camps.

We were pleased that we had performed well in our first action and were happy to relax and rest again at Camp Curtin. Once again, we could visit Harrisburg and enjoy the hospitality in that good city.

Only minor activity was conducted by our forces against the Confederates from August to November. One engagement did occur in December, 1861, that encouraged our Bucktails. At Dranesville, Va., we fought a strong force of Confederates commanded by Brig. Gen. J.E.B. Stuart. The battle was a small one in number of troops engaged; however, we defeated the Rebs, and they retreated in disorder. Unfortunately, Lt. Col. Kane was seriously wounded. Like many good officers, he tended to expose himself too close to the lines in order to get a first hand view of the action. He was carried to the rear for transfer to the hospital. Few other men were wounded or killed. We were told that the battle was considered the first victory for the Army of The Potomac.

We felt that we had proved ourselves to be able to handle anything the enemy could bring to bear on us. We chuckled when someone mentioned a "three month war," however.

Winter weather presented such difficulties in movement that operations on both sides slowed to a standstill. The regiment settled down for the worst part of the winter at Camp Pierpont near Harrisburg. Many of the men were able to get home for a few days, and my friends and I were among that number.

When asked by my folks in Ceres how soon we thought the Confederates would be defeated, I replied, "Your guess is as good as mine. Our officers think we are much better organized now, and when good weather arrives with spring, we should be able to dominate the war with our superior numbers. However, those Rebels show no signs of being ready to quit, so who knows how long it will go on?"

Throughout the spring and summer of 1862, the regiment was involved in several battles. Confederate Gen. "Stonewall" Jackson had been running roughshod over Union forces in the Shenandoah Valley of Virginia. Our company was included with Companies "C," "G," and "H' to reinforce Gen. Banks in the valley in an effort to curtail Jackson's shenanigans there. We formed part of what was called, "Bayard's Flying Brigade," fighting up and down the valley in a series of small battles. We had some success in reducing Jackson's raids, and we were reunited with the rest of our regiment after the loss of the second battle of Bull Run by Union forces in July, 1862. We were saddened that Lt. Col. Kane was wounded again and also taken prisoner while our forces were fighting in the valley. Everyone hoped he would recover and that he would be exchanged in the near future.

In September of 1862, we were part of the 5th Corps, Army of The Potomac, commanded by Major Gen. George B. McClellan. Gen. Lee's Confederate Army of Northern Virginia, including Gen. Jackson's troops, marched up the Shenandoah Valley shielded by the Blue Ridge Mountains to the east. Our forces were to shield Washington and were to move northwest in an attempt to destroy Lee's invasion of the north.

After a battle at South Mountain in Maryland, Lee moved his army near the little town of Sharpsburg, Md., aligning it in a north-south direction west of Antietam Creek. McClellan hurriedly took up a position on the east bank of the creek in a line almost five miles long.

Gen. Hooker's Corps, of which our Bucktails were a part, was located on the northern end of the line. Our company was back of the line on September 17th preparing an early breakfast.

It all happened quickly. We heard a bang like a clap of thunder. The first Confederate shells cut through the tops of the pines above us, showering us with limbs, bark and pine needles. The second barrage was right on target. One second Ed was leaning against a tree eating bacon and eggs; the next second he was gone – killed by a case shot that had exploded five feet from him. He was still holding his fork as if he had paused to take another bite. We had been shielded by the tree Ed had been leaning against. The rest of us had no injuries, except for a temporary loss of hearing. We had a hard time believing Ed would no longer be with us. Alex covered him with a blanket as the shells continued to come across our position.

Another man in our company screamed and grabbed his leg. It was Dawley and a shell fragment had broken his leg below the knee. Alex, Cliff, and I picked him up and carried him back to a hospital tent not far from our position. We saw other wounded men arriving there as the Rebel artillery grew in intensity. Dawley thanked us for helping him. We raced back to our position just in time to get the order to move forward. The whole Union line was in motion, and we advanced into a wooded area held by Gen. Hood's Confederates. Our artillery was responding, and the noise combined with the musket fire was deafening. At times, the smoke was so thick we could not see each other, let alone an enemy to shoot at. When the smoke lifted enough to crawl forward, we were pinned down by intense enemy rifle fire. It was awkward trying to reload and fire from a prone position, but it was the only way to do it and stay alive.

The battle raged on all day. The advantage changed hands several times. Our position for a long period was in what had been a ripe corn field. The corn stalks had been leveled by rifle fire so extreme that it appeared as though the corn had been cut by a giant scythe.

Terrible fighting also occurred along other portions of our lines, along a sunken road, and at several stone bridges where a desperate fight resulted in hundreds of killed and wounded when men of Gen. Burnside's IX Corps finally forced a crossing of the lower bridge. It was in the face of Rebel riflemen firing down on them from higher ground.

When the day ended, total Union casualties were over twelve thousand with Confederate losses in excess of thirteen thousand. One of the officers on Gen. McClellan's staff said he thought surely this would be the bloodiest day of the war!

Gen. Lee's army retreated across the Potomac and down into Virginia. It was not pursued by McClellan even though he had not committed all of his available divisions and had more reinforcements approaching. He decided that the Union army had been too badly crippled to attack again – much to our President's disgust and that of our officers who informed us.

In the evening with an end to the firing, a stillness settled over the battlefield. It was comforting to have a quiet time. Cliff, Alex, and I retraced our steps back to where Ed had been killed. He remained where we had left him under a blanket. The stretcher bearers had been too busy caring for the wounded to worry about the dead. We buried Ed and erected a wooden marker. I made a small map of the location in case his folks wanted to take his remains home for burial at a later date.

We also visited Dawley in the field hospital. He was in some pain with his leg, but admitted the doctors had been too busy with amputations and other seriously wounded men to give him much attention. He said, "I thank you guys again for your help in getting me here. I could have bled to death waiting for help out where I was hit. Who knows, I may be able to do the same for one of you, but I hope it doesn't come to that. By the way, you remember Sgt. Carey from "H" company? He saw you drop me off here and said you shouldn't have left your position to help me. That bastard is making a bad name for himself in the Bucktails. He's got a lot of enemies and most of them aren't Confederates. He'd better watch his back 'cause I'm not the only one who might miss my target, if I get returned to duty, that is."

We remained in the Sharpsburg vicinity for several weeks while the army licked its wounds and resupplied. The pause was good for everyone both physically and mentally. I considered myself lucky not to have been wounded. Cliff and Alex had lost some hearing, and we all had cuts and bruises. We tried to avoid talking about Ed's death.

Since we were among the able bodied, we were assigned to the details required after any battle. Our "working parties" picked up rifles, ammunition, cartridge boxes, belts, swords, and various pieces of clothing that had been abandoned. We assembled mounds of usable equipment that was stored for use again. Much of what we scavenged was common to both armies and was used until it wore out.

My friends and I also shared in the gruesome work that none of us enjoyed. We formed burial parties that roamed all over the field of battle collecting bodies and pieces of what had been men. Arms and legs were often found yards away from the corpses – the result of the terrible effectiveness of the canister and grape shot fired from the cannons. We matched

Drifting To Glory

up the body parts the best we could. Identification was very difficult as no standard system had been set up by the government to identify a soldier. Those men who could be identified were loaded on wagons, and taken to an area of high ground on the edge of Sharpsburg where a cemetery was established. Also, groups of "unknowns" were buried in common graves in the cemetery. Most Confederates were buried where they fell. Many men were buried in mass graves or deep ditches. Some of the higher ranking Confederates had markings on their graves which would help their relatives locate their bodies for a reburial in their home states later.

Hundreds of horses had been killed. Many lay on the battlefield in a wounded condition and had to be shot. The carcasses were piled in heaps and burned. A stench of dead men and horses began to fill the air after a few days, and burial efforts were increased. Some civilians offered help.

Confederate dead were seldom found with shoes on their feet. The Rebs were notoriously short of footwear, even this early in the war, and shoes were reclaimed by those who had worn theirs out. A Rebel who could find a pair of boots from a Yankee officer felt himself very fortunate. Even if they were not his size they could be traded for some that did fit or swapped for other goods.

Many men of both armies would go through the pockets of the dead. I was guilty of it myself. The practice was frowned upon but was common. We couldn't use the Confederate money, but the Rebs were glad to get their hands on our bills as our currency was accepted north and south. Gold coins were the most desirable, of course.

One of the more amusing scenes I witnessed while we were collecting bodies was that of a young Union private who came across what he thought was a dead Confederate captain. The officer was stretched out on the ground with his sword still in his hand. The private began unbuttoning the officer's coat pockets when the captain grabbed his arm and said, "Son, you try to rob me and I'll cut you to ribbons with this sword!"

The startled soldier jumped up and said, "Excuse me sir! I'll go find some help for you." He ran off looking for a stretcher bearer.

Our men were generally better equipped and fed than the Confederates. The Rebs were happy to help themselves to any hardtack, sugar, and especially coffee or tobacco that they could find in our haversacks.

In a wooded area close to where we had fought, I heard a whispered cry for water. I located a Rebel private who had been wounded in the right arm.

Drifting To Glory

He had lost a lot of blood, but thirst was his main concern. I gave him some water from my canteen and told him to try to stand up if he could. The man was too weak to stand and walk, and I said, "Wait here and I'll be back with help." I realized how stupid that must have sounded, especially when the soldier replied, "I'll be here. I have no plans to go anywhere."

I hurried back to our area and got Alex, and we rounded up a stretcher. We were back with the soldier in a few minutes. In spite of his pain he said, "Where have you been? I figured ya'll stopped for lunch somewhere." We had to laugh and placed him on the stretcher, delivering him to the hospital area. Before we left, he told us his name was Richard Mull and that he was from Chase City, Va. He hoped his arm was just bad enough that he'd be sent home, but not bad enough to lose it. He thanked us and we wished him well.

We looked in on Dawley to see how he was. He was asleep, but the aide said he was doing fine and would recover. He would be returned to duty in a few weeks as soon as his leg was healed. We were all glad he was doing all right, but were saddened to learn of so many Bucktails who had been killed or had serious wounds.

I wrote a note to Ed's family. We all signed it and the captain said he'd include it with his letter to the family.

The fall leaves turned beautiful colors as the Army of The Potomac like a huge, exhausted gladiator, slowly regained its strength on the hillsides surrounding Sharpsburg.

Drifting To Glory

Chapter VII

We were allowed passes into Hagerstown and Frederick, Md. while the army rested and resupplied at Sharpsburg. We chose to visit Hagerstown since it was a little closer. Cliff, Alex, and I piled on a wagon crowded with other men headed that way. We decided to look for a nice restaurant where we could eat something other than standard army fare. After asking some local folks, we learned about a good restaurant on Prospect Street. We were told it had good food at reasonable prices.

A short walk led us to a restaurant with a sign over the door which read, "Burnett's Restaurant." We were greeted at the door by a lovely girl in her teens and seated at a table with a pretty front window view. The young lady gave us each a one page menu and said, "You gentlemen look over what we serve. I'll be right back for your orders." She sashayed over to other tables to wait on more bluecoats that had followed us into the place. The menu listed fried chicken, chicken and dumplings, steak, and fresh trout. We could have coffee, tea or milk, and various pies and cakes were outlined as dessert choices. We were quite anxious to order when the pretty young lady returned. Everyone ordered fried chicken. The girl said it would be about a thirty minute wait for chicken. We were willing to wait.

In the meantime, an older woman came by our table and said, "Good day, gentlemen. I'm Olivia Burnett and I am the proprietor of this establishment. We've provided good meals here for almost twenty years, and if you aren't pleased with anything, you let me know. My husband, Jim, is a captain in the 148th Pa. Infantry which has formed over in Harrisburg. He told me to be sure to make any soldiers welcome who visit us, with the possible exception of Confederates," she said, smiling. "You know, we could hear the cannons firing during the terrible battle at Sharpsburg. We prayed for you all. Oh, here comes my daughter, Lillian, with your coffee."

We looked at her daughter with expressions of surprise. Alex remarked, "You don't mean to tell us this girl is your daughter? Why, she looks more

Drifting To Glory

like your sister than your daughter!"

Mrs. Burnett was obviously flattered by the remark and smiled politely. I thought I'd have a little fun with her, and said, "Now Mrs. Burnett, you know it's not ladylike to tell little stories about how young you are."

She was quick to reply. "Sir, it is the truth. Lillian is my daughter, and we are often mistaken for sisters."

"Well, we're certainly astonished," I remarked, "and I imagine compliments like that sometimes help to reduce the size of the bill." Alex and Cliff laughed at my joke. They slapped the tables, and several folks at the nearby tables laughed, too.

"You have made a gallant attempt young man, but the meal is still going to cost you fifty cents. I'll give you the dessert free, however." This brought on more laughter from the surrounding tables, especially from the other soldiers.

Apple pie was the dessert of choice, and when we finished, we were ready to loosen our belts. It was a delicious meal.

When we paid our bills, I asked Mrs. Burnett if the pies were made in the restaurant. She said her sister, Ruth, made all the pies and cakes, and was her main cook. We could see her flitting about in the kitchen. Mrs. Burnett added that the cookies on the tables were made by a friend – a Mrs. Doris McNew. She said Mrs. McNew is quite well known around town as the "cookie lady."

We looked at one another, and I asked, "Is she the wife of Sergeant Ray McNew?"

Mrs. Burnett responded, "Why, yes, he's her husband. Do you know the sergeant?"

"I guess we do," Cliff said. "We're quite well acquainted with the sergeant."

"Yes," I said, "tell her that we no doubt owe our lives to the good training her husband gave us up at Camp Curtin."

"I'll certainly tell Doris. You boys please be careful and come back to see us again. If you should meet my husband, please introduce yourselves and tell him you were here."

We left the restaurant and walked down the street a ways when a man in civilian clothes came up behind us. He said, "Good day to you, troopers. Bet you were in the thick of it at Sharpsburg, huh?"

Alex smiled at him, saying, "Yes sir, we were about as thick as you could get, I guess. What can we do for you?"

The man said, "It's more like what I can do for you. I'm Sherman Thompson, veteran of first Bull Run. I lost my arm there as you can see – can't do much, but I do what work I can to get by. I just thought I might steer you young defenders to a little entertainment, now that you got your bellies full. If you wanna play some cards, get something to drink, or maybe partake of some other entertainment, I'll give you directions."

"Heck, we might like a card game," I said. "Which way do we go? I think we could use a little liquid to hold down all that food. An after dinner drink would go just right."

The man looked pleased and said, "Walk on down Prospect Street until you see a great big house on the corner of Prospect and Washington. It has a big front porch with red curtains at the windows. Go up and knock and a lady will answer. Tell her Sherman sent ya."

"Thanks for the directions," Alex said.

"Don't mention it. I'm sure you'll have a good time."

We strolled down the street enjoying the sunshine. A brisk breeze was blowing bits of paper and dust along the ruts in the road. A fine coach passed us with two officers and their lady friends. The ladies were laughing and waved to us.

We crossed the street and walked to the corner as we had been directed. The house had been well kept and had a nice boardwalk along the street and leading up to the porch. The steps and porch had a recent coat of dark gray paint.

Our knock was answered by an attractive middle aged lady, very nicely dressed and smelling of expensive perfume. "Good afternoon, gentlemen. I am Aurelia Landingham. You may call me Mrs. Landingham. What brings you to my home, pray tell? I don't believe I've met any of you before."

We stepped inside as she held the door open for us. "Well, ma'am, a Mr. Thompson told us we might find a card game here, and maybe something to drink," I said. "He thought we'd enjoy ourselves, and we are ready for a little pleasure."

Mrs. Landingham smiled broadly and spoke, "We try our very best to entertain our guests, especially you boys in blue who are defending our homes from the southern invaders. Let me show you around. We are quite proud of our little establishment." She gestured toward two huge latticed doors through which we could see tables with poker games in progress. Women were gliding about, serving drinks and passing out cigars, making the men feel right at home. It was difficult to see clearly due to the pall of blue smoke hanging over the tables. We were reminded of the smoke on the battlefield, except it wasn't quite as noisy. Most of the men were soldiers, but a few civilians were sitting in at the games.

Mrs. Landingham turned around and pointed out a large parlor across the hall. Off the hall was a winding staircase which appeared to lead to small rooms upstairs. Red, white, and blue bunting hung everywhere in a garish show of patriotism. Our hostess opened sliding doors to the parlor. Several young women scantily dressed in various items of bright attire were lounging about the room. A young black man was playing the piano in the corner of the room. Two of the girls were dancing around and laughing at themselves as they circled the room.

"Ladies, ladies, please give me your attention!" The piano player stopped as Mrs. Landingham clapped her hands, and the women looked up attentively as she spoke. "These fine young soldiers have come to visit with us, and I want you to show them the utmost courtesy and kindness. Gentlemen, allow me to introduce my friends." She gestured with diamond adorned fingers, pointing out each girl saying, "This is Selma, Clarice, Adah, Naomi, Virginia, and that shy, sweet, little person on the end is Camille. She just recently came to stay with us. We have a few other girls who are tied up at the moment." The girls all smiled politely and waved.

"Now, gentlemen, please make yourselves at home and chat with my girls. They will be happy to tell you all about themselves. If you do care to play cards, we'll see if we can squeeze you in at the tables. I'll be in my office across the hall if you need anything. Goodness, there is so much paper work involved with running a business these days." With pettycoats rustling, she swished quickly out of the parlor, closing the doors.

I smiled at Cliff and Alex, saying, "Isn't she something?" We sat down on the ornate davenports with the girls nestled up close to us. The piano player resumed his playing in the corner of the big room. Cliff mumbled something about making ourselves comfortable, and our thoughts about playing cards were forgotten. We tried a little dancing.

I made some small talk about the weather, and started dancing with Clarice, a bewitching little charmer with flaxen hair and blue eyes. She was a good dancer and I felt clumsy.

Drifting To Glory

Cliff and Alex casually mentioned the war, and Selma waved her hands back and forth. "Let's hear no more talk about the war, and all the terrible things that are happening. We keep hearing about killing and bloodshed, and we just want to talk about happier times. There is a young soldier upstairs right now who had us all in tears, just to look at him. The army should send that poor boy home before he sees any more war. He looks so frail."

Our conversations began to wind down. Three of the girls we had been chatting with the most led us out of the parlor. They suggested we might like to see the upstairs portion of the house. As we passed Mrs. Landingham's office, she looked up, smiled, and gave us a little wave.

Upstairs, we entered separate, tidy, little rooms. The girls gave us the details of the usual financial arrangements for our visit. After having enjoyed all the "entertainment" we could handle, we were dressing when a hurried knock came at our doors. Virginia had rushed upstairs from the front entrance. She was out of breath as she told us we would have to leave at once. She spoke as rapidly as she could, saying, "There is a lieutenant and some soldiers from the Provost Marshal's Station. Mrs. Landingham doesn't know this new officer. He is arguing with her about soldiers consorting with undesirable companions or something. He wants any men in uniform out front right away, or they are coming in to look around. This hasn't been a problem before, but you'd better go to the window right this second and let yourself down with that knotted rope. Someone will be in the alley to help you." She disappeared down the hall.

The alarm was passed to each room, and in a minute or two, there were eight soldiers in the alley. Some of us were only partially dressed and carried our remaining clothes. We were not too surprised to see our one armed friend, Sherman Thompson, sitting on a wagon, ready to come to our aid. As we rushed to get on the wagon, the girls waved goodbye and told us to come back when we could. I waved and said in hushed tones, "Clarice, throw me my shoes!" I caught them just as Sherman slapped the horse with the reins.

The wagon lurched down the alley and into the main street to safety. Sherman left us where we could be picked up later by army wagons. We all laughed about our narrow escape. I said, "This is one visit to town we'll probably never forget, but I doubt we'll be telling our grandchildren about it." We all gave Sherman some coins for rescuing us!

Drifting To Glory

On the way back to camp, the army driver pulled off the road to allow the horses to drink. We hopped out, too, as it was a good, clear spring with cold water. I drank my fill, and said, "I like milk and coffee, beer and wine, but when you are really dying of thirst, there is nothing like a good cold drink of water."

Alex and Cliff agreed. So did a drunk soldier behind us who struggled to say, "I'll drink to that!"

Chapter VIII

New men and supplies arrived daily during the cessation of activity by the army at Sharpsburg. Our Bucktails had received new rifles before the battle. Most of us thought our casualties would have been higher had it not been for the new weapons. They were breech loading Sharps rifles and were far superior to what we have been using. The rifle could be fired at a rate of up to ten times a minute, or three times as fast as the old muzzle loaders. The extra firepower increased my confidence during battle.

The new replacements listened intently as we "old timers" passed on the details of the bloody Antietam battle. As we met men of a new platoon, I would look at Cliff and Alex and remark with a loud voice, "Well, look here, seems like we have a new supply of 'cannon fodder' to feed the Rebel artillery!" The new men smiled, but they didn't think it was much of a joke. We also referred to the young recruits as "fresh fish." They were coming into the Federal forces at a slower pace than previously. The newspaper accounts of the appalling losses were beginning to have an effect on new enlistments everywhere.

I wrote letters home more often than I had in the past. We all loved to receive mail and discovered that we stood a better chance of getting letters if we wrote a few. It was sad to see men show up for mail call and get no letters.

Alex received a letter from a girl named Carolyn McCain. She was one of the girls we had met at the party held for us in Williamsport, Pa. They had become good pen pals, and Cliff and I kidded Alex about the possibility that he would pass up going home on his next furlough in order to visit her.

Alex retorted, "You guys can laugh if you please, but at least I know a girl who writes regularly, and I can look forward to seeing her again one of these days." He looked at me, knowing that Karen had quit writing to me since she was engaged to marry a friend back in Ceres.

"You've got me there, Al," I replied. "I wish you good luck with Carolyn. I can't argue with the truth."

We suspected that the horrible fighting at Antietam had been more of a draw than a victory, especially when the casualty numbers were tallied and published. According to our officers, the battle did halt Lee's invasion of the north, however, and the President considered it the "victory" he had been waiting for to issue his Emancipation Proclamation, freeing the slaves.

President Lincoln visited the Antietam battlefield in early October to confer with Gen. McClellan and his staff. When I heard about it, I rushed back to our bivouac area. "Guess what?" I said. "I overheard some officers saying that old 'Abe' will be reviewing the troops tomorrow. The Bucktails are to be one of the regiments to march in review!" We spent the rest of the day cleaning and polishing our uniforms and equipment. In the morning, we were very proud to march past our Commander-In-Chief. It was a highlight in our army services that we knew we would never forget.

One other result of the President's visit was that he replaced Gen. McClellan with Gen. Ambrose Burnside. Most of the men hated to see "Little Mac" leave because we liked him and knew he had looked after our best interests; however, it was common knowledge that the President was disappointed in his failures to move the army. He was looking for a general to attack and win battles with the superior numbers of men and equipment we had on hand. The remark made the rounds of the camps that Lincoln had said, "Tell Gen. McClellan that if he is not going to be using the Army of The Potomac, I would like to borrow it for a while." After being inactive for weeks on end, we could understand how the President felt.

During our inactivity, we visited several adjoining camps and were astonished at the numbers of foreign troops in the army. Most regiments were composed of ten companies of about one hundred men each. We walked down company streets where we found that the entire regiment was made up of German immigrants, most of whom could not speak English.

We were surprised to learn that the majority of twenty Federal regiments were composed of Irishmen. Other regiments included Englishmen, Canadians, Frenchmen, Swedes, and Negroes. The diverse regiments brought with them their traditions, language, and often some variety of foreign uniforms. It was no easy task to form these troops into a cooperating, and coordinated Union army, but eventually we fought side by side.

Gen. Burnside reorganized the Army of The Potomac. In November of 1862, we moved south near the Fredericksburg, Va. area. Our general hoped to attack Lee's Army of Northern Virginia before the winter weather arrived. The Confederates were well entrenched on an area of high slopes called Marye's Heights along the Rappahannock River. The attack was badly organized and was a disaster. One common soldier said he thought we might as well have been trying to take Hell!

The Bucktails formed on the left flank of the army and succeeded in crossing the river. We moved up the slopes against Gen. A. P. Hill's troops under Stonewall Jackson. After passionate fighting and terrible losses, we were forced to retreat back north of the river. Many dead Union soldiers were found with their names and home towns written on notes, pinned to the backs of their coats. Knowing how futile the attacks were, none of us had little hope of survival and wanted to be sure our bodies were identified for burial.

We were happy to remove the identification from our coats and congratulated ourselves on being alive and all in one piece. It had been close. Alex and I had tears in our uniforms where minie balls had passed by; Cliff had the heel of one boot shot away and was limping on that foot.

I grinned and said, "I guess the Three Musketeers have been spared once more. We slipped and fell down so much that I believe we missed the minie balls that had our names on them. Seriously, I'm getting sick of all the useless waste of life we're always subjected to by generals who can't decide how to whip a smaller army."

Cliff added, "Yeah, I agree. I just wonder how many more leaden pills the Rebs are going to feed us before they make one or all of us sick."

We understood Gen. Burnside actually planned to renew the attack the next day, but on the advice of his staff who considered it insane, he opted to fall back between the Rappahannock and Washington to shield the capital from danger for the winter.

The opposing armies settled into winter quarters by late December. Along with other troops, Co. "I" dug rifle pits and built small log cabins or huts to protect ourselves from winter weather. Many of these "homes" were quite elaborate. The Bucktails were skilled at felling trees and made use of their rubber blankets, or "gumcloths," for roofing material. Many

Drifting To Glory

homes such as ours was built with a glass window. We chinked logs with mud and tar. We had a heating stove made of discarded tin sheets. We used the same stove to cook on and dry clothes. Small logs were used to make a floor, rather than have dirt to walk on, which would coat everything with dust, including our food. Also, a dirt floor became a mud bog when heavy rains flooded the campgrounds. Lumber became very scarce.

Small things made the huts more livable. We made a book rack and table out of old box boards, and stuck our bayonets into the walls to use as candlestick holders.

Naturally, the army set up guidelines for the quarters to be laid out. They spelled out the dimensions of camp streets, where the kitchens, sinks and latrines were to be located, and where the baggage trains should be parked.

The officers had finer accommodations. The higher ranking officers had houses just for themselves while others shared their homes. Some officers' wives and children visited the camps and spent days with them.

We were stretched out on our bunks one evening after chow. I said, "I always get a kick out of how we refer to Gen. Burnside as 'old sideburns' with those heavy muttonchops on his cheeks. Since we call ourselves the Three Musketeers, if we were to grow big mustaches we could call ourselves the 'Three Mustachios'." I looked at Cliff and Alex to get their reaction. Cliff rolled his eyes, and Alex shook his head.

Alex said, "That cinches it! You get one arm, Cliff, and I'll grab the other, and we'll drag him to the dispensary. This guy definitely needs help now. No sense waiting 'til sick call in the morning." They wrestled me out of my bunk and dragged me outside.

"I hope this cold air will help clear your head," Cliff said. We laughed and stood outside a minute, smelling the fragrance of the pine knots that were burned to help light the company streets. Then we went indoors for the night.

I sat on my bunk and was quiet for a moment. I said, "Guess it would be best to remain as the Three Musketeers. On the other hand, I'm damned tired of shaving…just might grow a mustache after all."

Furloughs were not often granted, and this Christmas season was no exception. We had just fought at Fredericksburg on the thirteenth of December. The army was busy funneling new replacements into the ranks of the regiments which had lost so many men. Ours was included, and new men had to be trained. Because of this, we were very surprised when the first sergeant dropped by to tell us we could get a three day pass for the Christmas holiday. Christmas fell on a Monday, and we were given passes for Saturday, Sunday, and Monday. Evidently, our officers had gone to bat for us. Everyone knew that there was no chance of any military action, especially at Christmas. We appreciated the gift no matter how it had come to pass.

Our camp was not far from Warrenton, Va., and from there it was about forty miles to Washington. We decided to go to Washington on our passes, but couldn't afford three days there, so we spent Saturday in camp. We brushed our uniforms, used some soap and water where needed, and shined our shoes. We spent the remainder of the day resting in our hut, playing cards, writing letters, and staying warm.

We discussed the noticeable improvement in camp life. The U.S. Sanitary Commission had come into being not long after the start of the war. Included in its objects was the raising of hygienic standards of our camps and diets. Our officers were instructed to have us maintain the latrines with adequate dirt covering. We were also urged to wash our hands before eating and to keep our clothes and quarters as clean as we could. It was believed the incidents of typhus, dysentery, and malaria were lessened considerably by these steps. We were told to discard old or dirty food items.

Our diets were responsible for much of the diarrhea that was so common. It was recommended that the camp cooks use less fat and bacon grease in cooking and serve less fried foods and the great army staple – fat salt pork. Vegetables were showing up more often in our meals.

One advantage in getting away from camp was always the opportunity to get some different meals. We thought about that as we prepared to leave for Washington. It was a dark, dreary morning with overcast skies that held a promise of an improvement. At least the wind was calm, but we took a scarf and gloves in case the weather took a turn for the worse.

Wagons had been leaving the field hospitals with wounded men since the battle. They would take those who were able to move to hospitals in the Washington area. We didn't think we'd have a chance to get in one of those wagons – they were usually loaded to capacity – nor did we relish the idea of riding with wounded men who would rather not have company. We succeeded in climbing aboard artillery wagons carrying field pieces needing repair or other material from the battlefield. The wagon trains stretched all the way to the capital. It was not a very comfortable ride, but our discomfort paled by comparison with the jostling of those who were wounded or ill.

Washington was decked out for the Christmas season. Wreaths, boughs, and bunting decorated the streets and gaslights. When we arrived in town, we thought we'd be wise to try to locate a place to spend the night on Christmas eve. A representative of the U.S. Christian Commission advised us it was futile to try to find any rooms at a hotel. No rooms available anywhere in the city at this time of the year. After all, Washington had been busy since the war had started without the complications of a Christmas crowd.

We decided to worry about a place to sleep later. We could always sleep in a back alley somewhere if we had to. It couldn't be much worse than some places we had slept since we had been in the employment of "Uncle Sam."

It began to snow. The flakes were big ones...the size of dimes, and they floated leisurely to the ground since there was no wind. They added to the Christmas atmosphere.

We stood on the street corners watching the parade of people bundled up against the weather. Buggy drivers were having a hard time weaving around the people who stood in the street and talked. It appeared that every third person was one of us! Blue uniforms dominated the fashion parade.

We were used to eating at a regular time in camp, and our stomachs reminded us that the time had arrived. Although the restaurants were crowded, we were able to enter one of the cheaper places; in fact, the proprietor made room by moving a couple tables together. Our chairs were with a young second lieutenant. He was a new officer and wore his gilded straps proudly on a spotless uniform. His name was Lt. David Preble.

As we ate and discussed the war, he asked where we were stationed, and when we told him he replied, "Well, I'm stationed much closer. I'm at the War Department, and not only that, my home is right here in the capital."

He was very interested in where we had fought, and before we got ready to leave, he asked us where we were spending the night. I said, "At the moment I think we'll find the best spot we can in an alley somewhere."

He replied, "I know how crowded the city is, but I think I can help you do a little better than an alley. It might not be much better, except that it will be cleaner and dryer. My folks have just added a new stable behind our house and even have some new hay laid out. The horses are boarded elsewhere until next week. You are certainly welcome to spend the night there, and we have plenty of blankets." He laughed and added, "I just had a funny thought. I have two older sisters. I'm going to tell them in the morning that I offered to let two of you sleep in their rooms, but since there were three of you, it wasn't fair to make one of you sleep alone in the stable, so you all decided to sleep in the hay. If you knew my sisters, and you'll meet them in the morning for breakfast, you'd think what I said was pretty funny, too."

We laughed with the lieutenant and thanked him for the offer. It was a ten block walk to his home, and all things taken into account, we had been pretty lucky to have a stable to sleep in, and a new one at that. As the young officer bid us good night and wished us a merry Christmas, I was reminded of another scene. I said, "This is a strange coincidence, sir, at least in part. Here it is Christmas eve. A long time ago the bible told the story of Mary and Joseph finding no room at the inn and having to sleep in a stable. It seems kind of honorable to sleep here tonight."

Lt. Preble smiled, saying, "It does seem odd now that you mention it. Hope you all rest as well as can be expected under these circumstances. See you in the morning for a good Christmas breakfast."

"There goes an officer I'd like to have in our company," I said. "He'll probably be fortunate enough never to see any combat, except fighting with people at the War Department."

"Speaking of good fortune, how lucky have we been today?" Cliff asked.

"I'll tell you in a minute," Alex said, "as soon as we flip a coin to see who gets to sleep in the middle where it'll be the warmest."

Drifting To Glory

Chapter IX

In the morning, we met Mr. and Mrs. Preble and their daughters, Mary and Lee. We were invited to have breakfast with the family and were pleased to accept the invitation.

When the lieutenant introduced his sisters, he smiled at us. We noticed the girls blushing and realized he had mentioned his joke about the sleeping arrangements.

"We're pleased to meet you gentlemen," Mary said.

"Yes, we're glad you were able to stay with us," Lee added, "and hope you slept well considering the primitive sleeping accommodations." She smiled politely at her sister.

Mrs. Preble said, "Yes, it's a shame you couldn't have slept in the house, but we are short of space at the moment."

We noticed the girls smiling and blushing again. The lieutenant was having a difficult time keeping a straight face. Alex, Cliff, and I smiled and went on eating.

"What are your plans for this lovely Christmas day?" Mrs. Preble continued. "The snow has stopped falling and the sun is shining brightly. Doesn't seem to be very cold today."

Mr. Preble decided to join the conversation as he finished his coffee. "I don't know if David told you, but we are not long time residents of Washington. I am the senior senator from Wisconsin. We've lived here for ten years. I thought perhaps you might like to ride around the capital with David and the girls. I can have the carriage brought around, and our offspring can show you the main points of interest. You could return this evening to share our Christmas meal. We'd enjoy having you with us."

"We're certainly flabbergasted by so much hospitality," I said, "especially when we're strangers in your home."

"Oh, please don't feel that way," Mrs. Preble said. "We are very proud that you are helping to defend your country, and any small thing we can do is nothing by comparison."

We passed the afternoon very enjoyably. The weather was still cold enough to keep the streets from becoming soft and muddy. It also gave Cliff and me an excuse to snuggle up close to Lee and Mary. Alex was content to drive the team pulling the carriage while the lieutenant pointed out the historic buildings along the streets.

"I guess we need to be getting home for our Christmas dinner," the lieutenant said, as he instructed Alex where to turn back to their home. "And by the way, you guys can quit calling me lieutenant...'Dave' will do quite nicely."

"Yes," Mary said, "you'll have him feeling like a major or something when he's just our little brother."

After a sumptuous dinner of turkey with all the fixings, we paid our respects to Mr. and Mrs. Preble. They asked us to return at our first opportunity.

Dave and the girls drove us out to the road that led back to camp. "I'm worried that you may have some difficulty getting any transportation back to your camp on Christmas night," Dave said. "I know medical wagons have been running day and night, but they may have slowed up today, especially. We'll drop you here, and hope you're able to make it back to camp for muster in the morning."

I said, "We'll wait here a while, and if no wagons come along soon, we'll start walking. At least we'll keep warm and will be heading in the right direction."

We shook hands with Dave and thanked him for his kindness. The three of us hugged the girls, and they asked Cliff and I to write. They knew Alex would be sending his letters to Carolyn. We watched their carriage as it disappeared in the darkness, wishing that it was not so far back to camp.

A few wagons arrived in the city as we waited, but none departed for an hour. We stamped our feet, rubbed our arms, and finally decided we might as well hit the road as stand there half frozen. Thank goodness we had sense enough to bring the gloves and scarves. It really didn't seem too bad...walking along at a brisk pace with no rifle or pack to carry. We told stories, jokes, and recounted the things we did as kids. We talked about the girls we had known, both good and bad.

It got colder and the wind started to get stronger. The snow crunched under our feet as it does when it's dry and very cold. There were no stars now, and we began to have trouble staying on the road, such as it was. The cold was bitter, and the thought of freezing to death along the road was not the least bit appealing. I said, "I think we're in a pickle, and a frozen one at that. I figure we've walked for five hours and made maybe twenty miles, but we've got that much more to go. If we ever see another wagon headed for the city, we'd better get on it and go back to Washington. We can turn ourselves in for overstaying our leaves in the morning and take our medicine. I don't know what else to do."

"Beats freezing to death out here," Cliff said.

Alex just mumbled and pulled his coat collar around his face again, adjusting his scarf around everything but his eyes.

Twenty minutes passed, and hope surfaced once more. We saw a wagon moving slowly toward us from the city. We shouted and hailed the driver who wondered what on earth we were doing out in the middle of nowhere. The wagon was full of medical supplies and mail. We rearranged the load to make room for our numb bodies and made good use of the hospital blankets for the rest of the trip.

Thank goodness we weren't required to fall in for muster until eight o'clock on the day after Christmas. It gave us two more hours of sleep beyond what we have been able to get in the rough wagon ride.

We discussed our "expedition" to Washington during breakfast. We'd make better plans next time. We enjoyed getting away and meeting the girls, but cursed the frozen trip home.

Drifting To Glory

Chapter X

We celebrated the beginning of 1863 in camp. We were not permitted to fire our weapons in camp, except in rifle practice, and severe penalties were handed out for such actions. The penalties could range from a few days confinement, to "bucking and gagging." This amounted to the prisoner being gagged with a stick in his mouth, the soldier seated on the ground with his hands tied in front of him. Then his knees were pushed up between his elbows, and a stick was forced between his arms and knees, pinning him in a dreadfully uncomfortable position. After a few hours like this in a hot sun, a man never repeated firing his rifle in camp, or broke any other rules!

So, we celebrated the coming of 1863 in ways that did not usually lead to punishment. Enlisted men were not permitted to have alcohol on a military base, but officers received a daily ration at most posts. Some of this alcohol made its way into the enlisted ranks, and men often smuggled booze into camp when they returned from leave. We had a small amount on hand which was sufficient to celebrate in a sane fashion. As long as we didn't go overboard, and make a lot of noise, we were safe. Unfortunately, drunkenness plagued the armies on both sides throughout the war.

We got in a serious mood as we sat around our fireplace as the new year arrived. Cliff said, "By, do you think '63 will be the last year of the damned war?" Alex rolled over on his side in his bunk to listen to what I would say.

I poked at the condition of the fire before answering. "I don't know anymore about it than anyone else, but at the rate this army is making progress. I have grave doubts about an end before our three year enlistments are up! It makes me wonder if we'll have enough men to finish the job, or if any of us will still be around when it is finished."

Cliff agreed, saying, "Wouldn't it be a kick in the ass if most of the troops who are here to accept 'Bobby Lee's' surrender are boys who have not yet even entered the army?"

"That would be a damned dirty deal," Alex said, sitting up, "especially when guys like us will have done the bulk of the fighting!"

"Someone please deal the cards," I said, changing the subject. "It doesn't help to try to think too far ahead."

Pvt. Dawley shared a hut not far down the company street from ours. We had let bygones be bygones since our fight back at Camp Curtin. Also, Dawley hadn't forgotten that we'd carried him to the field hospital when he was wounded at Antietam. Dawley liked to play poker and checkers and became a frequent visitor at our hut.

The regimental commanders knew that it wasn't wise for us to sit around with too much time on our hands; therefore, we continued to drill and fall in for inspections and present our rifles for inspection, too.

We laughed at one private who summed up the routine: "The first thing in the morning we start to drill. Then we drill and drill some more, followed by drill. Then we drill, drill again, and finally we finish up by drilling."

The weather could be depressing. Days of freezing temperatures and overcast skies became monotonous. We had a variety of ways to help keep our spirits up. We played cards until we wore them out, played checkers, chess and gambled with dice at a game called chuck-a-luck. Others played faro and other games of chance. Most men would bet on anything. Cock fights were popular. Baseball games and boxing matches were held and were a source of wagering. Raffles were often held. We even saw men betting on which of two lice would be first to reach the opposite side of a stretched out blanket!

We visited the sutlers' wagons where they sold "dime novels," bibles, newspapers, candy, tobacco, fruit, and just about anything we could afford. Shoes, shirts, socks, and other clothing items were available – all at inflated prices.

Men who were talented at wood carving turned out some beautiful work. Letter writing was a popular pastime, and old letters were kept and re-read several times. Anyone who could play a musical instrument or had a good singing voice was always in demand. A crowd quickly formed anywhere when several soldiers showed up with a fiddle, banjo, guitar, or concertina. Occasionally, a regimental band would entertain us with a concert and play the popular tunes of the day such as: "Annie Laurie," "Tenting Tonight," "When This Cruel War Is Over," and "The Battle Cry of

Freedom." Music was a big morale booster, and we loved to tap our feet, clap, and sing along. I learned one song was not played as often as others at the concerts. Several officers asked the band leaders to refrain from playing "Home Sweet Home" because they felt that it could have a demoralizing effect on the troops, most of whom were homesick enough without hearing that song.

I jokingly suggested to Cliff and Alex that if we could learn to play an instrument we could hold our own little concert on the company street, and the guys might throw small change at us. Cliff laughed at the idea and said, "Yeah, I'm sure they would throw a lot of things at us, but I doubt any of it would be money!"

Good news arrived from the western theater of the war that improved our morale. Newspapers received in January 1863 reported the Federal success at the Battle of Stones River at Murfreesboro, Tn. Although it was a tactical victory for the Confederates, Gen. Bragg was unable to drive the Union forces under Gen. Rosecrans from the field. Bragg elected to retreat to the south, making the campaign a Confederate failure.

During an informal meeting in the Bucktail camp, one of the officers remarked, "Well, if we can't dislodge 'Bobby Lee' from Virginia here in the east, at least we seem to be able to move against his forces in the west. They say Gen. Grant is determined to move south even though we seem unable to do so."

A captain from Co. "F" rose to speak. He said, "You know, soldiers, I've also heard that we are beginning to get some very effective help from our sea-going brothers in arms. The U.S. Navy has launched more fast ships to intercept the Rebel blockade runners that have been bringing in supplies from foreign nations to southern ports. I understand the purpose is to gradually strangle these imports and reduce the flow of arms, explosives, medical supplies, and foodstuff the Rebs are badly in need of. Over the next few months, the flow of these war materials will be reduced to a trickle." He smiled as he added, "If we can just keep the Rebs from capturing so much of our war materials, the blockade will become very effective, indeed!" His remarks were greeted with applause and hurrahs from all of us gathered around him.

"I have one more item of news for you that has just come down from headquarters. For what it may be worth to you men, the President has relieved Gen. Burnside and replaced him with Gen. Joseph Hooker." Most

Drifting To Glory

of us cheered, but a few just shook their heads. "Hooker can't do any worse for us than old 'sideburns' did at Fredericksburg," the captain grimaced. We had to agree with that.

Gen. Hooker hoped to justify the President's confidence in him and also wanted to better morale among his soldiers.

We saw the effects of his efforts in short order. In an attempt to increase pride in our individual units, the general instituted a system of corps badges to be worn on our caps. The badges were stamped out of flannel cloth, and since we were part of the 3rd Div. of the 5th Corps, our badge was a blue maltese cross. It was not an important detail, but it did give us some recognition and set us apart from other units.

Our officers told us that Hooker was straightening out the quartermaster, commissary, and medical departments. Rations improved and the camps were cleaned up to the extent that our health improved. It was noted that fewer men went to sick call, and the scourges of diarrhea and dysentery began to decrease. Filthy conditions in our camps were improved, and we were required to use the dirt "sinks" and latrines rather than answering nature's call behind our tents or huts or anywhere we felt like it.

Gen. Hooker got rid of troublemakers, both in the ranks of enlisted men and officers. We noticed a general shake up in our officers and non-commissioned officers. One mistake in judgement was noted, however, when we learned that one of our sergeants was transferred and replaced with the hated Sgt. Carey of Co. "H." How that happened we never knew, but we all vowed we'd do our best to stay out of his way.

In camp, we now had regular church services, and the sutlers had an improved class of wares although prices always remained high.

Small camps arose outside the confines of the military boundaries. In these establishments, liquor and gambling were available to those who could afford it. Prostitutes plied their trade, and men took advantage of this "horizontal refreshment" as it became known. The men started referring to the prostitutes as "Hooker's girls," or just "hookers." The general tried to curtail the businesses by the various "camp followers," and the activities that went on outside the camps, but it was felt that a controlled amount contributed to morale. We learned that passes outside of camp were not handed out freely.

Chapter XI

It had been a severe winter. It was late March before the weather and roads had improved enough to prepare for the spring campaign. By mid April, Gen. Hooker moved the army south of the Rappahannock River and west of the bloody scene of battle at Fredericksburg. With upwards of 130,000 men, he planned to destroy Lee's army once and for all.

Our new general did no better than his predecessors, however, and did not press the tactical advantages we held. Lee outmaneuvered our army as in the past and won the battle.

Chancellorsville was a brilliant victory for the Army of Northern Virginia, and Federal losses were very heavy. We soon learned that Gen. Lee had sustained a loss that he was unable to replace, however. Stonewall Jackson was shot by accident by one of his own men and died a few days later. The newspapers outlined that Lee had lost his "right hand."

Gen. Hooker had come close to being a casualty when he was stunned by a shell that exploded nearby. Some men joked that they wished the shell had been much closer.

The Army of The Potomac was withdrawn to safety north of the Rappahannock again. Our Bucktail companies had fought in another difficult battle that was not successful for the Union. We were bitter about being "out-generaled" again by Lee and were beginning to believe our generals were all stamped out of the same piece of moth-eaten cloth!

One soldier took it all in stride when he said, "It seems for every step we take forward, we take two backward. One of these days we're going to reverse that trend and find ourselves in Richmond."

Articles in our newspapers outlined that Washington believed the Confederates hoped another victory would help to obtain military support from England. Flush with the success at Chancellorsville, the Confederates embarked on another invasion of the north. It would help relieve our pressure on Vicksburg, Ms. and Chattanooga, Tn. by drawing Union forces away from those cities to oppose Lee's forces as he came north. Lee started north on June third, 1863, and moved his army away from the Fredericksburg area, westward into the Shenandoah valley. Shielded by the Blue Ridge Mountains, the long lines of troops and wagons proceeded northward as they had before the Antietam battle.

Lee's veterans were in good spirits. In addition to their own supplies, they had tons of munitions and foodstuffs captured from us at Chancellorsville. They were traveling through friendly territory and picked up some recruits along the way.

Hooker's reconnaissance operations noted the Confederate movements. Several small cavalry battles were fought ahead of the main units. Hooker pushed our army into motion, being careful to shield Washington from any surprise thrust by the Confederates. Our forces moved parallel with the Rebel forces as they moved into Maryland where Hooker concentrated the closest corps of our men near Frederick, Md.

The Union Chief of Staff, Gen. Halleck, countermanded some of Gen. Hooker's orders, and we lost another general when Hooker asked to be relieved of command.

Major Gen. George Meade was quickly appointed to succeed Hooker. He had commanded the Fifth Corps of which we were a part, and we hated to lose our corps commander, but we were all delighted that he would now command the entire Army of The Potomac.

The Confederates poured out of the valley, and spread out over the green Pennsylvania farmlands. This was as far north as they had struck in force, and the residents were very alarmed. So was our new commander of the Army of The Potomac, and Meade hurried to get the remaining army corps moved into position. Many divisions were still a day's march south.

The first contact our troops made with the enemy was when the Confederate Heth's division of A.P. Hills' corps marched into the little town of Gettysburg in search of a supply of shoes reported to be there. They made contact with Buford's Federal cavalry. Neither army had their main forces on line yet, and the first day's fighting was won by the Confederates. Our forces suffered a serious loss with the death of Gen. Reynolds.

The Confederates moved through the streets of Gettysburg, capturing the little town from the north, while the Federal army positioned its forces on the south of town, the line resembling an inverted fish hook with the eye of the hook resting on two hills south of town called the "round tops."

Our Bucktails, now under the Fifth Corps commander, Gen. Sykes, had been held in the defense of Washington. We were now ordered to the support of the army in Pennsylvania and had to march much like Stonewall Jackson's so called "foot cavalry" in an attempt to get to the field of battle in time. We arrived about noon on the second day of July and were immediately pressed into battle near the "round tops," and a very rocky area called the "Devil's Den."

This practice was repeated often during the war. Men tired from forced marches were required to swing into action, often without food or rest, and we found ourselves in this position upon our arrival at Gettysburg.

We became engaged at once with the Rebels of Gen. John Hood's division. The rattle of musketry filled the air with noise and smoke. The noise reverberated among the rocks making it hard to hear commands. Cliff, Alex, and I were firing from a higher elevation than most of the company among the boulders of the Devil's Den when Cliff hollered, "Come over here, By!" I scrambled over beside him as he pointed out a Rebel sharpshooter lying on a boulder in the bushes about forty yards from us and below our elevation. "The bastard is trying to pick off our officers with his fancy rifle. You're the best shot. Get him quick before he moves out of sight."

I refused, saying, "You saw him first – he's all yours."

"He ain't worth fussing over," Cliff said. "Let's both shoot him before he gets away!"

"Fine with me," I answered. We both raised our Sharps and fired. The Reb dropped his rifle and rolled off the boulder like a log.

"That's one less we have to worry about," Cliff said.

I smiled grimly and answered, "The killing is getting easier, isn't it?" Cliff just nodded as we reloaded.

The Confederates began to fall back a little in the face of the musketry we were pouring down on them. I heard Sgt. Carey yell at us to move on down the slope to get closer to the new Rebel positions. I noticed at the time the sergeant refrained from getting any closer than he had been.

I took up a new position, almost where the Rebel sharpshooter had been. His body was still there. He looked as if he was taking an afternoon nap, except for the bullet hole in his head and the blood oozing from his side. I assumed both Cliff and I had hit him.

Drifting To Glory

The Rebel had picked a well covered position, except I was firing in the other direction. Down the slope from my vantage point, I could see enemy riflemen beginning to reform for another attack on our positions. They came charging up the slope, in and around the rocks, hollering that Rebel yell we had heard so often. It was not really disturbing, but it always raised the hair on the back of my neck when I heard it.

I shot the first man who came around a large boulder, and the second who was right behind him. I thought the flow of men would stop when they saw the bodies piling up in front of them, but they just continued to advance as if the men who had been shot had lain down to catch their breath. They kept advancing and I kept shooting as fast as I could reload and fire. The smoke formed a ragged cloud among the rocks, and the noise was deafening. I wondered if I'd be able to hear anything after this uproar was over.

I couldn't suppress the feeling that I was enjoying what I was doing. I no longer wondered if killing other men was right or wrong. It had become mechanical, and I had become very efficient at my task.

Many of our men had expended all forty rounds of ammunition in our cartridge boxes, and we had been scrounging around in the cartridge boxes of the dead and wounded for more. We were relieved to see the Rebels falling back once again. They broke off the counter-attack, retreating across a little stream and through a wheat field.

Our lines extended to the north along cemetery ridge and swung east to Culp's Hill. We could hear firing in the distance to the north and knew serious fighting was occurring there. We hoped our men were giving a good account of themselves, but we had our hands full. It was all we could do to keep from being overrun by the Rebs on our end of the line.

Now the Confederate artillery got into position and began to shell our lines. Artillery shells were exploding in the air and among the boulders of the Devil's Den area. We had to hold our hands over our ears which were already stuffed with pieces of cloth or cotton. We could still hear the hissing sounds of shells passing over us, exploding behind our lines.

I could see the smoke from our twelve pounder "Napoleon" field pieces. Occasionally, a perfect smoke ring would form, like those we would try to perfect with a cigar. Other puffs of smoke, for some strange reason, would remind me of the round biscuits mother used to make on the stove. I guess you think of strange things under the pressure of the moment.

Drifting To Glory

The Confederate artillery ceased, and we braced ourselves for the renewed infantry assaults which came immediately. The Rebels were trying to dislodge our forces from the hill called "Little Round Top" and attacked with wave after wave of infantry. The brunt of their thrusts was received by regiments from Maine, Michigan, Pennsylvania, and New York. The Rebels were finally driven off the slopes of the hill, falling back to the wheat field and a peach orchard near the Emmitsburg Road. Ammunition on both sides had been nearly exhausted, and our forces had used their bayonets to effect the repulse.

The Bucktails continued fighting as skirmishers in the Devil's Den area. Smoke drifted in and out of the trees and boulders. I was lying in a shallow gully starting to reload my rifle when a Rebel infantryman appeared out of nowhere. He evidently was among several men working their way back to their lines among the rocks. He glared at me angrily, moving forward with out hesitating. He had a confident manner about him as if I was a piece of work he had to complete before going back to his lines. He moved at me brandishing his rifle with fixed bayonet. I got to my feet, trying to remember the bayonet drills we had been through. I knew it was now or never, and as he lunged at me with his rifle, I sidestepped to the right. Before he could swing back at me for another attempt, I swung to my left and thrust my bayonet into his side. He groaned and fell to the ground, trying to extract the bayonet with his hands. I could tell he was losing consciousness and put my foot on his chest and pulled the bayonet out of his ribs. He just stared at me with glassy eyes and died in that moment.

I had no idea what had happened to Cliff and Alex and was starting to search for them since we had a lull in the firing. Before I moved from my position, an artillery horse suddenly staggered into the area, dragging a broken harness. As he stumbled before us, we could see that he had been badly wounded with grape shot or canister. His entrails were hanging from a gaping hole in his side and were dragging on the ground. A wounded officer saw him and said, "Someone shoot that poor damned beast!" I raised my rifle and shot the horse in the head, ending his suffering.

We listened to the weak sound of a drum, thinking we were to assemble for another forward movement, but the cadence was that of a slow march. Out of a wisp of smoke came a Rebel drummer boy, flanked on each side by riflemen as they came slowly forward. Now, I saw Alex. He shot one rifleman who fell on the boy, knocking him to the ground.

Someone shot another infantryman, and the rest of their squad took cover behind the rocks, moving out of range. The boy got up, replaced his cap, adjusted his drum, and came forward as if nothing had happened. He marched right up to us, still beating his drum, with tears streaming down his face. He was obviously dazed and would have kept marching right on up the hill. I grabbed his arm and spoke gently to him, "You're one of the bravest soldiers we've seen today. Here, sit down, and have some water."

He took my canteen eagerly, and said, "Thank you very much, sir. I haven't had a very good day so far, and now I guess I'm your prisoner, too."

"Guess so," I said, as I put my hand on his shoulder. "Come with me and we'll make arrangements for your surrender." I led him back of the lines and turned him over to an orderly. "See that this soldier is fed a good meal. Give him to one of the officers for safe keeping until things quiet down, and we can get him exchanged." Later that evening, he was escorted under a flag of truce to his own lines.

As the afternoon passed, we were located at the foot of "Little Round Top." The strategic hill had been held and was well fortified with cannons. Under Gen. Hood's command the enemy had been attempting to take the hill all day with repeated infantry attacks in great force. Hood was wounded and lost the use of his left arm. We finally drove the enemy back for the last time late in the day and took up positions along a stone wall east of the wheat field. We had taken many prisoners and field pieces before the Rebels could remove them. Our company lost a dozen men, and the regiment suffered the loss of Col. Taylor. He was killed instantly, just before we halted our drive. Since Lt. Col. Niles had been wounded, the regiment was now commanded by Major Hartshorne.

The second day of battle had ended with the Confederate attacks repulsed on the Union left flank. Our lines on the northern portion of the battlefield had held their positions and beaten back attacks at Culp's Hill and at Cemetery Ridge. Darkness ended the day's actions. Men on both sides tried to rest as much as possible. Fires were built and coffee was made in great quantities. Beef, beans, and bread were brought up from behind the lines, and army food had never tasted better. It had been a long hard fought day, and most of us had not eaten since breakfast. Many were not on hand to eat and would never eat again. I wondered as we looked at one another how many of us would be available for supper again tomorrow night. No one brought up the subject for discussion.

A familiar looking soldier came shuffling into the light of the camp fire. "My God if it isn't Sgt. McNew!" Alex exclaimed. "We figured you had finished training the boys in blue and had gone south to help train Rebel recruits."

"Not funny, hayseed," the sergeant replied. "They have sent me here knowing damn well you nincompoops would need some guidance, and someone to wipe your noses. They knew I was good at prodding malingerers and slackers into action."

He grinned at us and we laughed at what he had said as I asked him, "Seriously, sarge, how did you get here?"

"I didn't exactly put in for it," he answered. "When the word came down that Lee was headed this way, they just about cleaned out Camp Curtin...left only a skeleton crew to play nursemaid to the very newest recruits. I never told you, but I spent a couple years with an artillery brigade back in the fifties. They told me to hunt up Battery "C" of the 4th U.S. Artillery. It's here with the Third Division, Second Corps, under Gen. Hancock's command. That's where I've just reported in. It's up in the center of the line, and knowing that Lee tried our right, and then attacked our left – against you guys – I know sure as I'm talking to you, tomorrow he'll attack our center with all he's got left. You wanna tag along and see some real action?"

"We sure would like to come give you a hand, sarge," I said, "but that artillery ammunition is damned heavy, and those field pieces are hard to move. I think we'll just work with these little Sharps cartridges. They're so light and easy to handle – guess we're just a bunch of spoiled slackers."

"I knew I couldn't depend on you greenhorns," McNew said.

"Oh, by the way, sarge," I said, "before I forget it, we ate in a restaurant in Hagerstown where your wife supplies the desserts. They sure were good!"

The sergeant laughed. "My god – the army doesn't have enough problems with the Rebs. Now my wife is trying to poison our troops!"

We laughed as we got up to shake hands with our former sergeant. "Good luck to you fellas tomorrow," he said.

"Same to you, sarge," we answered. "Give 'em hell," I said.

With the remaining hours of the evening, we cleaned our weapons, and washed up as much as conditions permitted. We stuffed some hardtack and

Drifting To Glory

dried beef into our haversacks with the thought that we might not be in a position to get anything to eat during the next day.

The dead that were within our lines were moved to the rear and laid out in rows for burial as soon as possible. The main priority now was for our army to strengthen its position and resupply the ammunition. The conference Gen. Meade had with his staff resulted in the agreed decision to remain on the field and fight the next day. Additional units of the army had arrived during the day, and the Army of The Potomac was holding the best position it had held since the war began.

As we sat around our campfire, we talked about the day's fight. We agreed if Lee pressed the battle tomorrow, it would be a decisive battle.

Cliff and I wrote short letters to our families, and Alex wrote to his folks and Carolyn. Cliff remarked as he sealed his letter, "I don't think we need worry about attaching our names to our blouses like we did at Fredericksburg. I believe the scales are going to tip in our favor on this one, although I have to give Lee's troops credit. Those 'secesh' fought like a storm from hell today without a doubt."

"There's sure nothing lacking with the Rebs' spirit and determination – just hope we can match 'em tomorrow," I said.

We looked across the lush fields at the flickering campfires of the enemy. I imagined those men were thinking about home and loved ones and if or when they might see them again. We were all much alike, but just aligned on opposite sides.

A partial moon cast an eerie, blue haze over the scene of the day's battle. The quiet was in stark contrast to the clamor of battle we had experienced only a few hours ago.

We knew we should get some sleep and many men had no trouble dozing off after the long marches and exhausting fighting, but I sat up for a while chatting with Cliff and Alex.

It was too hot to sleep in our tents, and some men sat or stretched out on their bed rolls and smoked. We could see the little red glows of the cigars and pipes. We lit up some cigars, too, and gazed at the bright stars wondering if we'd be alive to see those same stars on the next night.

A private close to me spit out a stream of tobacco juice. I told my friends, "You know, I've tried it, but I can't stand that plug tobacco. Don't believe I could ever get used to it."

Cliff was amused and said, "Ah, By, that plug tobacco is good for you.

Drifting To Glory

If you swallow enough of that juice it will make a man of you and put hair on your chest." He paused for my reply.

"If that's the case," I said, "I guess I'll have to remain a bare chested lad." Alex smugly bit off a small plug and smiled.

Someone shouted, "How about you guys piping down so we can get some shuteye?" We knew that was a smart idea and lay down for the hours remaining. The last thing I heard was a pack of dogs barking in Gettysburg more than a mile from our position. The barking ceased and started again as a nervous picket on vedette duty fired at an enemy shadow.

We were awakened by our bugler sounding reveille. A quick vision of a stray bullet – from either army – flashed gleefully through my mind. It would be more humane to just steal the bugle and bury it, but I'm sure the army had plenty of bugles. They'd just requisition another for that damned horn tooter.

Chapter XII

The battlefield was relatively calm on the morning of June third with the exception of the Culp's Hill area on the northeast section of the lines. Here our Union forces had finally defeated a strong thrust by the Confederates to take the hill. It was about ten-thirty in the morning. The entire battlefield area appeared eerily quiet as if both sides were trying to decide what to do next.

We rested at our positions and drank from the extra canteens of water which had been brought forward. I chewed nervously on dried apple slices I had in my haversack and prayed this would be the last big battle. We were all sick and tired of this stinking "three month" war.

Both sides had prepared for the larger battle that was expected to come in the center of our lines. At about one o'clock, two Confederate signal guns fired, and then, more than one hundred artillery pieces of all types opened fire from a line two miles long on Seminary Ridge. Union men who had been lying on the grass resting after lunch, instantly jumped to their feet and took up their positions as the shells started falling among them.

Hundreds of birds took flight at the frightening sound of the explosions. They left the lush green forests of the round tops, not to return until after nightfall. Many men wished they could take flight, too, and some made the attempt, only to be rounded up by officers and returned to their lines.

Some of the shells fired from Whitworth breech loading cannons made a peculiar hissing sound as they passed overhead. The Union generals were surprised at the magnitude of the Confederate barrage and described it as the heaviest fire they had ever experienced. Over eighty cannons from the Union batteries quickly answered the Rebel fire from the center of the Union line. Additional guns fired from our left flank, close to our position. Many additional guns were held in reserve behind our lines. Gen. Hunt, in command of our artillery, felt that he could use no more than eighty guns to our advantage since our line was shorter than the Rebel line.

The artillery duel continued for almost two hours creating a cloud of smoke obscuring the lines. Shells were fused to explode in the air and on impact with the ground. Both sides had difficulty seeing their targets, and each side tended to fire high. This was more of an advantage to our side because the Confederate forces appeared to be massing infantry behind their lines for an attack, and many shells fell among them killing dozens of men before they even began to move forward. Much destruction occurred, however, on both battle lines. Men, horses, caissons, and limbers were blown to pieces. Horses broke loose and ran frantically around the lines. Some horses threw their riders and ran off, not to be seen until after the battle.

Many men were dazed by the repeated concussion of exploding shells and sat or sprawled on the ground, staring into space. I felt very nervous as I held my ears and shut my eyes during the height of the explosions.

During the cannonade, our regiment was holding its position along a low stone wall near the wheat field. We periodically exchanged shots with Rebels on their right flank and who never gave up hope of attacking and turning our flank.

The thunder of the artillery could be heard for 100 miles. Everyone who heard the noise in the surrounding cities and villages hoped and prayed the battle was going well for the Union. About three o'clock in the afternoon, the Union guns ceased firing to allow the guns to cool and to conserve the ammunition.

The Confederates believed they had possibly silenced the Union guns, or that they had become short of ammunition. Gen. Lee therefore ordered an infantry attack to go forward. Approximately fifteen thousand men in ten brigades formed in dressed lines stepped out smartly from Seminary Ridge. Their regimental flags fluttered in the light breeze, bands behind the lines struck up martial tunes, and everyone on both sides admired the beauty of the advance. **Their objective was a small clump of trees in the center of our lines.**

The Union artillery waited a few moments and then resumed firing, tearing gaps in the beautifully dressed lines. The gaps were quickly filled with other men and they pushed on. Gen. Pickett had initiated the charge at Gen. Longstreet's direction, and he exhorted his men to press forward steadily for the Federal lines without hesitation.

Drifting To Glory

We could see the long advancing lines much better now from our vantage point, and although their right flank was at least a quarter mile from us, we were ordered to fire into the mass of men without any individual target.

Union artillery continued to devastate the long gray lines, and as the Confederates got closer, additional guns were brought to bear on them from the lower end of Cemetery Ridge and from the elevated positions on Little Round Top. These batteries enfiladed the lines with terrible effect. As the ranks came within short range, the Union guns were charged with canister, firing small steel and lead balls about an inch in diameter, much like giant shotguns. Union riflemen began a withering fire which added to the carnage. Many of our men had as many as four loaded rifles on hand and all had at least two. This gave us additional firepower when needed. Everyone had extra percussion caps and bullets.

The reality of war was delivered in full force to men of both sides who had never known war before. The rattle of muskets, the shouts of the soldiers, and the screams of the wounded and dying filled the air – pandemonium prevailed!

A portion of the attacking force reached the small clump of trees and a low stone wall, and at this juncture, the fighting became hand-to-hand. Men used bayonets, knives, rifle butts, and their fists as weapons. The artillerists fired point blank charges into those groups of men who had not quite reached the wall and were splattered by the bloodshed they had caused. The attack slowed as officers and men died intermingled with those of the opposite side. Union reinforcements quickly filled in the gaps in our defense, and the Confederates fell back. They had given their very best, but it had not been enough in the face of the strength of the Union forces. Hundreds of them were taken prisoner, and others who had not been badly hurt helped their wounded comrades back to Seminary Ridge. Some men who had not surrendered were killed or wounded trying to retreat over the long mile back to their lines.

The Confederate attack had reached the "High Water Mark," and now nothing more could be done, except to try to save those who were still alive. The attack had cost Lee over five thousand killed or wounded in less than thirty minutes.

Longstreet began to reorganize his men for a counter-attack, but it never materialized.

Drifting To Glory

The Union forces had repulsed Lee's attack, but we had been seriously hurt, too. More Union forces had arrived on the field, however, and the Confederates were in no position to renew the fight.

After Pickett's charge, the Bucktails had been ordered through the wheat field and into the woods southwest of it. We succeeded in driving the enemy, capturing many prisoners.

The Rebels fired several twelve-pounders at us before they retreated on our section of the field. Alex was advancing several yards ahead and to the left of my position and Cliff's. We heard the shriek of a shell coming close. Shell fragments filled the air as the case shot exploded.

Alex hollered, "I'm hit!" and fell on his back. Cliff hurried to him and could see Alex was in pain, but couldn't see a wound. I came up just as Alex said, "It's my left hand. I think part of it's gone."

"His hand is covered with blood," Cliff said, "but I don't see the wound."

"There it is," I said.

"Where? I still don't see it. Is it a cut?" Cliff asked.

"No," I said. "It's his little finger. It's gone!"

"Well I'll be damned. Shot off clean as if cut with a knife. A surgeon couldn't have done better."

Alex blurted out, "If you guys will help me up, I think I can get back where I can get help to stop the bleeding.

A sergeant arrived and quickly wound some cloth around Alex' hand. "I've learned to carry some clean cloth in my knapsack for little occasions like this." He grabbed the arm of a young private passing by, and said, "You help this man to the rear, and get him some attention."

The young private was sweating, and his face was smeared with black powder stains where he had been tearing cartridges open. He smiled and said, "Gee sarge, I hate to miss the action up ahead, but I'll do it to help a wounded man."

"Yeah, I know just how much you hate getting off the firing line and going to the rear where you can get a cool drink and a bite to eat. Get going with him before I decide to take him myself." The private smiled again, and started to the rear with Alex. The sergeant shouted after him, "Don't forget to report back to your company when you've run your errand!"

We pushed on after the enemy until Major Hartshorne brought us to a halt. The enemy troops had fallen well to the rear, and we needed to see to our dead and wounded. We had lost a number of wounded and had several dead from our company. As we searched, I noticed a soldier lying flat on his stomach. As we approached him, we were surprised to see it was Sergeant Carey. We were also astonished to note he had two bullet holes in his back. We looked at one another and wondered how that came about.

I said, "I've got the strong feeling that the Sergeant has died for his country, killed by his own men!" Cliff and others were in agreement. Of course, we couldn't be certain, but we knew how the sergeant never got too close to the front lines. Also, we knew he had made a number of enemies in the regiment, several of whom would have shot him when the opportunity presented itself and never given it a second thought. Needless to say no one but his mother was going to miss him, and we couldn't be sure about her. We did know that no one would admit shooting him, and only God would know the culprit. He was taken away for burial and no investigation was made. Dead men had become too common.

The Confederates continued to fall back on all sections of the field. Gen. Meade was determined to engage them and follow up the success of the afternoon, but darkness effectively ended the action. The men of the Army of The Potomac were exhausted after long forced marches and three days of battle. We needed food and rest.

Even though the Army of Northern Virginia had been badly hurt, Lee waited on July fourth to see if Meade would attack. His artillery chief informed him that they had enough ammunition for one more day of fighting if necessary. The men of his army were still in good spirits and would be as long as Lee was there to lead them, in spite of having lost over twenty thousand men in killed, wounded, and missing. The losses to the Union were over twenty three thousand.

Gen. Meade learned from his signal officers late in the afternoon of July fourth that the Confederate army was starting a retreat. The wagon train of wounded was over seventeen miles long. Many wounded had to be left in makeshift hospitals at Gettysburg. Some Confederate doctors stayed with them. Thousands of wounded on both sides would have to remain at Gettysburg for weeks before they could be moved. They overflowed the local hospitals in the surrounding towns and were confined in local buildings such as the Seminary building at Pennsylvania college, churches, public buildings, warehouses, and private homes. Many of the slightly wounded suffered in the heat of field hospitals. Alex was among that number, but could at least move around.

Hospital trains were leaving Gettysburg at the rate of six per day by the end of July. Doctors came from hundreds of miles to help save the wounded of both armies.

The President had urged Meade to pursue Lee's army without delay and destroy it, but on the Fourth of July, a line of severe thunderstorms developed with rain falling all night. The weather aided Lee's escape and hindered our efforts to cut off his retreat. Meade moved cautiously, unsure whether Lee would stand and fight again. He kept the army between the Confederates and the roads to Washington.

Several sharp cavalry engagements occurred at the rear of the Confederate lines as Meade tried to engage Lee's army, but by July fourteenth it was too late. The Confederates had made good their escape into Virginia. Everyone was disappointed from the President on down the line to the Bucktails. According to our officers, the armies had fought what had been so far, the largest battle ever fought on the North American continent. It had been a victory for us, but it hadn't brought the war to an end.

Cliff and I met Sgt. McNew again before the various corps had refitted and replaced their losses in men and equipment. We told him about Alex's wound and where he was recuperating, and then we realized there was something new in McNew's appearance.

I exclaimed, "Well, I'll be damned. Will wonders never cease? Look at the shoulder straps, Cliff. The old sergeant has gone and become an officer on us!"

"Well, I'll go to hell if he isn't a new shavetail," Cliff said, pointing at the bright new shoulder straps.

"That certainly warrants a tribute," I said proudly, and we snapped to attention and saluted our former sergeant.

McNew beamed and returned the salute. "I invited you to join me in the middle of the line, but you preferred to play hide and seek in the rocks and trees. You both might have distinguished yourselves if you had pitched in and helped me out and become corporals or better." He smiled and became more serious for a moment. "I know you gave a good account of yourselves. You were good material for the army as recruits. I was just in the right place at the right time. I was assisting a battery of twelve-pounders when the Rebs dropped a shell on top of us. It only scratched me, but it killed two officers and badly wounded a gun crew. I was ordered to take charge of two field pieces, and we really poured the canister into that Rebel charge. They had come almost up to the muzzles. There were body parts scattered everywhere. Well, a Brigadier behind us was actually helping to pass ammunition to us and observed the whole scene. He gave me a battlefield promotion on the spot, and it was confirmed by his superior. I was one happy old sergeant." He laughed and added, "I'll probably go ahead and make the army my career. A second lieutenant is a good start."

We got a kick out of that and shook hands with him. I said, "If this war goes on much longer, you'll probably be a captain next time we see you." We saluted again as he strolled away wearing a big smile. We were happy for him.

The aftermath of the battle was a repeat of the scene at Antietam. Working parties roamed the battlefield and camping grounds of the Confederates picking up the normal assortment of small arms, ammunition, and all the other accouterments normally found in the residue of battle. Other crews tended to the wounded men who were still lying on the far flung corners of the huge area of battle. They also picked up the dead and pieces of the dead. Dead horses were dragged to convenient areas, piled up, and burned since it was too much of a chore to bury them deeply enough to prevent the stench of rotting carcasses. A large area next to the Union lines was set aside for burial of the known and unknown.

Many relatives of men killed at Gettysburg arrived to claim the bodies of their loved ones and take them home for proper burial. Undertakers did a thriving business in embalming the dead and advertised their services in the newspapers. It was usually the wealthier families who could afford this service.

We watched the hospital trains arrive and depart with their wounded cargoes. Many wounded died on their way home, according to the newspaper accounts.

It was also interesting to visit the areas where captured Confederates were being assembled for shipment to points to be exchanged. We were discouraged from visiting with prisoners, but did it anyhow when we had a little spare time. We enjoyed chatting with them and swapping stories of our experiences. Some men traded small amounts of coffee or tobacco for Rebel uniform buttons, or belt buckles and breast plates, and sent them home to family members.

One officer overheard a Rebel prisoner talking with us and walked over to hear what he had to say. The prisoner was proud of the gallant charge they had made on the third day and said, "Nary a one of us thought that we couldn't take your lines, sir. Gen. Lee believed in us, and we hate that we let him down this time. But he'll strike again like lightning, 'fore you blue bellies know what's hit ya!"

The captain took a long drag on his pipe before he answered. "Yes, private, I imagine he will, but you won't know the joy of being with him. I understand they're going to stop this prisoner exchange practice, and you can hear about your Bobby Lee's exploits in a prison camp someplace where I hope it's snowing."

The Reb prisoner frowned and knew he had been insulted, spat on the ground, and walked off without saying another word.

Chapter XIII

The captain addressed us at a company meeting a few days after the battle. He explained how much progress was being made in the conduct of the war. He smiled and said, "In the western theater of the war, the day after our success here at Gettysburg, Vicksburg, MS met the terms, and surrendered to U. S. Grant's forces." We cheered as he continued. "This came as very encouraging news to the army and the country. We believe we are on a down hill roll, and that the war will not last much longer. This will help with the enlistment of new men. Also, we have new and better equipment coming in the weeks ahead. The colonel asked me to congratulate you on your hard fighting on the field of battle, to keep up the good work, and we'll all go home sooner than we think."

We stood and clapped and shouted our huzzas. We had heard this type of speech in the past, but now we were getting evidence of actual victories, and we were encouraged.

Unfortunately, the captain was in error about the victories helping with the enlistment of new men. When the public was made aware of the casualties we had suffered, enlistments dropped off to a trickle. We had read in the newspapers that a Federal Enrollment Act had been passed in March of 1863, and in late July, the first draftees were being picked in New York. Resentment had been growing over the draft. It exploded into a four day riot in New York City which resulted in buildings being burned, businesses looted, and over one thousand people killed. Before it was stopped, Federal troops just back from Gettysburg were called in to quell the mob of over fifty thousand people.

We could not believe what we read. It seemed there was more fighting going on around the country than just on the bloody battlefields.

In early August, 1863, our army was camped again on the north side of the Rappahannock River in Virginia. We had spent so much time in the general area that we were beginning to feel right at home in Virginia. The

Drifting To Glory

Army of Northern Virginia went into camp at Culpepper, Va.

Also during August, Alex returned to Company "I". After surgery on his left hand, he had remained in a field hospital for several days. We asked what they had done with him after his surgery was completed. He answered, "Well, the doctors checked my hand a couple times a day, if they had time. They were pleased with my progress – no infection had occurred. They assigned me to light duty, bringing up small bundles of medical supplies. Several times they had me carrying severed arms and legs to wagons for disposal. I finally told them I was tired of the blood, and the smell of decaying flesh, and men dying just waiting for attention. I couldn't get used to doing that all day and said I'd rather take my chances on the firing line. The doctor in charge said he understood, and since my wound was healing quickly, he asked me if I wanted to go home for a few days."

"He was a pretty funny old guy. He said he had a notion to tell me he didn't think I was well enough to travel so he could keep me around a while longer – said he thought I might consider transferring to the medical department. I told him, 'Thank you very much, but no thank you, sir. I was glad to help out while I was here, but I hope I never come back here either vertically or horizontally, if I can avoid it.' The old doctor laughed at me, and admitted that he could see my point of view. Then he surprised me by saying he could arrange a furlough for me if I thought I could use one. I quickly told him I could use one very nicely, so I'm out of this garden of evil tomorrow."

"Heck, you've been away from us a month, and now you're going home on furlough. Cliff and I are beginning to think you've grown tired of our company."

Alex smiled and said, "It's not your company I've grown tired of, it's infantry Company 'I.' I'll get away any chance I can get, short of desertion."

We bid Alex good-bye and he was gone in the morning. He visited his folks at home and stopped by to see Cliff's and my folks. On his way back, he spent a few days at Williamsport renewing his friendship with Carolyn.

He was back in camp before we knew it and told us about his visits. He also surprised us with the announcement that he was going to ask Carolyn to marry him if he could get any more leave at Christmas. He thought it would be best to wait until the war was over to actually tie the knot.

Cliff and I were happy for him and agreed we thought it was best to marry after the war ended. It couldn't last much longer anyhow.

I told Alex, "We like your plans, except for one little item. Carolyn has been writing Cliff and me and says she can't make up her mind which one of us she wants to visit her at Christmas." Alex knew we were kidding, but acted like he didn't, and said, "Oh yeah, well put up your dukes, and I'll fight ya one at a time!"

I grinned at him. "Al, you know there's a policy against fist fighting in the regiment. You'll have to challenge us in the boxing ring, but right now let's put it off and go to chow."

Cliff added, "Yeah, enough of this tomfoolery. I always follow the policy of eat first, fight later. I always fight better after I've gotten some nourishment."

"Damned cowards," Alex said as he laughed at us.

We washed up and headed for the mess hall. This was a good evening. They had butchered some cattle, and we were pleased to have beef steak for a welcome change. Fresh bread had been baked, and we could smell it before we reached the end of our company street, called "Park Avenue."

In the morning, the company formed up, and we marched with the rest of the regiment toward the left flank of the Confederate lines. The Bucktails were back on skirmish duty for which we had earned a well deserved reputation. Sharp exchanges occurred almost daily between Union and Confederate pickets. When I mentioned the severity of these encounters to a new second lieutenant, he told me, "Ah private, these are a few minor engagements we are having."

I looked at my buddies and said to the officer, "Well, lieutenant, we never consider anything a minor engagement if we are being shot at and minie balls are whizzing past our ears. You can call it minor if you like, sir."

The lieutenant laughed. "I see your point, soldier. A man can be killed or wounded in a minor skirmish just as easily as he can in a major battle. I'm sure if I were to lose an arm or leg, that would be a major battle to me!"

The fall weather brought heavy rains. We had to slosh along in the mud which made marching miserable. The horses and mules had the same difficulties with heavily laden wagons on roads underwater which were almost "unnavigatable."

When thunderstorms rolled across our paths, and frequent lightning occurred, most companies would remove the bayonets from their rifles for fear that they would act like lightning rods. Some officers didn't think it made any difference and thought the lightning would strike where it wanted to, bayonets or no bayonets. However, they allowed us to sheath our bayonets if we wished and to carry our rifles at the "trail arms" position, rather than on our shoulders.

The armies seesawed back and forth across Virginia, gaining little in these maneuvers. Gen. Meade attempted to outflank Lee's army when he became aware Lee had weakened his forces by sending Longstreet's corps to Tennessee to aid Gen. Bragg's army in that theater. Meade's attacks were to no avail. The movements of the armies during the fall months passed the troops over the old battlefields at Bull Run and close to Centerville, Va.

Nothing was accomplished by early November, and Meade and Lee were back in their former positions. We camped in an old Rebel camp, which had been very well built south of the banks of the Rappahannock. The Rebels went into camp south of the Rapidan River on familiar ground.

Gen. Meade did not want to abandon campaigning for the winter without making one more attack on the Confederates. Near a tributary of the Rapidan called Mine Run, a new attack was planned. The area extended west of Fredericksburg, Va. We were slow to position our forces, and Lee perceived Meade's intentions and adjusted his lines accordingly.

The Bucktails were pushed ahead as skirmishers. As we attempted to cross a stream in a shallow spot, Rebel artillery began firing with good effect. We waded halfway across the stream, having difficulty keeping our footing due to the slippery rocks. An artillery shell exploded a few yards from us, sending up a geyser of water. I fell and Alex shouted, "There goes By!" He and Cliff rushed to me, expecting to drag my lifeless body to the bank of the creek.

I struggled to my feet saying, "Let go of me, damn it! I'm not hurt. When that shell exploded, it scared me so bad I slipped and fell in this damned icy water." Alex and Cliff thought this was very funny and roared with laughter, in spite of additional shells whistling overhead. We skedaddled to the relative safety of the high ground back of the creek.

As we were lying there, Cliff said, "You know, By, you really should do something about your language. You used to be a clean cut, straight laced, temperate young man. What's come over you these past months?"

I knew Cliff was teasing me and played along. "Oh, I think it is probably these nasty, little war games we've been playing at and losing." We clung to the ground as more shells hissed overhead and exploded out of range. "Actually, my swearing is not that bad. It's more of a feminine type." Cliff and Alex looked surprised as I went on. "Yeah, I use some occasional 'damns' and 'hells,' but that sounds like 'damsels,' don't you see? What could be more feminine and innocent?" I watched my friends for their response.

Alex said, "Evidently, the explosions have rattled your brain, By. Cliff, you keep an eye on him while I go find a stretcher to tie him to." We laughed even though we expected Rebel infantry to come charging across the creek following the artillery barrage. None came and we were ordered to fall back. For whatever reason, the Rebs decided not to attack.

As we shouldered our rifles and hurried back to our lines, I reflected on how much I had changed since I had left home. I've matured and hardened like everyone else, but I don't think I'm a worse person than I was. We've all killed in the defense of our country, but that's the task of an armed soldier – kill or be killed and do as you're commanded to do. When this cruel war is over, as the song goes, I think I'll be able to emerge with a good outlook on life.

We arrived back at our bivouac area. I looked at Cliff and Alex as we stacked our rifles, and said, "Well, buddies, we've just battled through another episode of the old normal, 'cold, wet and muddy'."

Drifting To Glory

Chapter XIV

Once again, by the time the Union forces had untangled their movements in the engagement, Lee was one step ahead of us. Operations for the year came to a halt, fortunately on a note of encouragement. News filtered down to us of the Union victory at Chattanooga by Gen. U.S. Grant. As we trudged through a fresh snowfall on the way to our mess hall at Bristoe Station, I remarked, "I wonder what Grant could accomplish if they were to let him try his hand with Lee here in Virginia?"

Cliff looked at me, shook his head, and said, "How could he possibly do any worse?"

No one was eating when we entered the mess hall. A very young captain – the officers seemed to be getting younger all the time – was standing at the front of the hall. He instructed us to sit as he looked over his notes, and spoke. "I have been asked to bring you up to date on the progress we have made as campaigning comes to a close. I'll be brief."

I nudged Cliff and Alex with my elbows, and whispered, "Uh, oh, I think we're going to get another victory speech!"

The captain began. "I know we've all heard of the great victory at Chattanooga by Gen. U. S. Grant. It was well received after our losses two months earlier at Chickamauga. We are now well established with a two theater war, and higher command believes the Confederates are not going to be able to continue to oppose our armies in both the west and the east. Coupled with the fact that our navy is blockading the import of everything they need to sustain the war, it is just a matter of time until they give up the struggle. You can be proud of the effort you are giving in smashing their resistance, and we ask you to keep up the good work. That is all I have to tell you at this time. Please enjoy your meal."

I cheered along with everyone, but added my own little comment. "I'm not really being pessimistic, but I'm puzzled as to what higher command defines as 'just a matter of time'. We could all be old and gray in 'just a matter of time'."

We were hoping the winter of 1863-64 would be the last winter of the war. Many civilians and soldiers began to think we should call a truce if the army could not win a decisive victory. A peaceful solution could be negotiated over the conference table instead of the battlefield. The Confederates believed the Yankees should let them go their own way, forming the separate government they had wanted from the beginning. The feeling became stronger as the casualty lists grew longer.

The winter was more severe than anyone could remember. I thought the snow piled up on our huts made them look more like igloos than cabins. We worked at making our "bomb-proof" dwellings more "storm-proof." Most of the men had built log huts like those of the frontier cabins. The cracks between logs were daubed with mud or tar. Some had dirt roofs on top of boards, others just boards covered with rubber sheets or thatched. Sometimes the earth was dug to a depth of a few feet to make the huts warmer and roomier. Most of them were occupied by four men, and we could keep plenty warm enough with fireplaces we fashioned from discarded metal drums, or bricks and rocks. We were getting resourceful at building living quarters. We were getting better with experience.

We had not been asked to take in anyone with us in our hut, so we had a little extra space for our gear. We figured the space would be taken up with a new recruit by spring.

As Christmas approached, Alex suggested we try to get furloughs and go home for the holidays. The furlough policy had become a little more liberal since there was little possibility of any major campaigning due to the usual problems associated with winter. It was as if a truce was in effect each winter.

Alex was determined to visit Carolyn again in addition to his folks. Cliff and I were anxious to go home, not so much to renew any friendships with old girl friends, but rather to get some good home cooking during the holidays.

We rode army wagons to Washington and boarded a train to Baltimore and Philadelphia. Pvt. Dawley and a few others from the Bucktails made the trip, too. Train transportation continued to Williamsport where Alex departed. He wished us merry Christmas and we asked him to give Carolyn our regards. We hoped she'd accept his proposal if she had been able to forget Cliff and me. He shook his fist at us and left smiling.

Drifting To Glory

A winter blizzard descended on our train not far west of Williamsport. The snow added to the drifts already across the tracks in narrow places in the hills. Unfortunately, the only way out was to return to Williamsport where the railroad helped to arrange rooms for the night. We decided not to stay and took our chances on horse drawn carriages and made it to Corning, N.Y. We were able to get a train westward to Olean across terrain that had much less snow.

We found so few young men in Ceres when we arrived that we were happy to help out with the chores around our homes. We helped the neighbors whose boys had not been able to come home. Ed Dodd's family was glad to see us and appreciated us stocking the bin behind their house with firewood. Few families had not been touched by the war. If a family did not have a son in the army, they had relatives or friends in uniform. My sister, Abigail, complained there were no men left in town between the ages of sixteen and fifty. Others who had physical problems, which kept them out of the army, had left town to work in factories producing war goods.

Everyone who was able attended a Christmas party at the Methodist church. A few speeches were made welcoming the men who had been able to come home. The names were read of those men who would never be coming home again, and the preacher expressed in prayer the wish that the next Christmas would find the nation at peace with all the boys at home.

Cliff and I planned a shopping trip to Olean to buy some gifts for our families, although we couldn't afford much on our thirteen dollar monthly pay. I pleased my sisters – Electa, Mary and Abigail – by inviting them to go with us. I told them I wanted to be sure they got a chance to buy me a present.

Olean was brightly decorated with festoons of leaves, boughs, and ribbons stretched across the streets. Sprigs of holly and candles of varied colors were in the store windows.

We attended a band concert where all the Christmas songs were played. A chorus of school children sang carols and such old favorites as, "Annie Laurie," "Sweet Evalina," plus "Tenting Tonight," and other military tunes – "When This Cruel War Is Over," and "Battle Cry of Freedom." The performance was concluded with an older gentleman reading Lincoln's Gettysburg Address. The audience stood and sang "The Battle Hymn of the Republic."

On Christmas morning, gifts were exchanged in front of the big fireplace at the inn. My mother had knitted gloves and a scarf for me, and I assured her they would get much use. I couldn't think of more useful gifts.

My father took me aside and asked me about the Gettysburg battle. I told him about the terrible casualties, and the confusion that occurs in battle with men occasionally shooting their own men. I shook my head and said quietly, "Father, I never expect to see any fighting as horrible as I experienced at Gettysburg and Antietam. The noise was enough to drive you crazy. I know I don't have normal hearing now even though we tried to protect our ears. Having come through those days unhurt, I hope if I'm lucky, I'll make it through to the end."

I told him about Alex's wound. I did not tell him about the men I had shot, and those I knew I had killed. It would have served no purpose, and I didn't care to think about it and dismissed it from my mind.

"We'll be thinking about you and praying for you, and all your comrades," father assured me. "You keep writing to us and we'll do the same. Your mother and I look forward to your letters very much."

Alex arrived from Williamsport the next day to visit his family and tell them about his engagement to Carolyn. He had written them so often about her that they were not surprised.

We talked of happier times. The women started to prepare supper at the inn where we had room for everyone. The girls had the main room looking like a store window with all the glittery decorations. A large spruce tree erected in one corner of the room was covered with a myriad of silver balls, various little, painted wooden animals, and a pretty angel on top that the girls had fashioned out of a little doll. They had added white feathers for wings and made a golden halo out of small brass wire. Popcorn was strung on thread and wrapped around the boughs several times. They placed some candles on the tree, but father insisted that they remain unlighted. He knew of friends who had suffered a disastrous fire when candles set their tree on fire and burned the house to the ground.

We would have to get the train in Olean in two days, so everyone wanted to have one last happy evening together. We sat around the big fireplace and talked after the scrumptious meal was finished. We had eaten so much we could hardly move. There were so many pies, cakes, and puddings that mother knew most of the women would have to take some home.

It wasn't long until the room was filled with pipe and cigar smoke. Mother knew some of the guests were very uncomfortable. She and father

Drifting To Glory

opened the front and back doors for a few minutes to allow the cloud of smoke to move outdoors. The cold air was refreshing and we all felt better, especially the women and children. A few small children and babies had dropped off to sleep and weren't bothered by anything.

A neighbor boy had brought his guitar. We sang Christmas carols and patriotic tunes until the fire burned low.

Drifting To Glory

Chapter XV

We returned to camp and learned in early January of 1864 that the spring campaign would begin after the first good week of improved weather.

Conditions at the Bristoe Station camp became more strict. Men and equipment were inspected more often. A general sprucing up of the regiment began in preparation for renewed activity.

One morning the Bucktails were told to fall in, and we wondered what was happening when Col. McCandless stepped out in front of us. He said, "I have good news for the Bucktails. Due to your past training and experience as skirmish troops, you are among the first soldiers to receive the Spencer repeating rifles that are now being produced in quantity." We jumped in the air, cheered, and slapped one another on the back. The colonel smiled and continued, "I don't know of any men who deserve these weapons more than the Bucktails. I'm sorry they arrived a little late for Christmas and have no red ribbons on them, but higher command thought you would understand and would appreciate them anyhow."

At last a change for the better. The new year seemed to be off to a good start. All the men had either seen the new carbines or had heard of them. It was a seven shot lever action repeating rifle. It loaded with a tubular magazine through the stock. It was lighter and shorter than the standard rifles we had been carrying, and fired an all metal, self contained fifty two caliber cartridge. The Rebels who had seen Union cavalry using them hated it, and called it that 'damned rifle that you could load on Sunday and shoot all week!"

President Lincoln had seen the Spencer and had fired it at least three years earlier and wholeheartedly approved of it. Unfortunately, the war department decided that the soldiers would waste ammunition using the repeater, and the production was curtailed for the first two years!

Since the Spencer was shorter, we wondered if it would be as accurate as the longer rifles. We began training with them, and it proved to be a little less accurate. Also, since the cartridge contained only forty-five grains of black powder, the gun lacked the range and muzzle velocity of the longer guns. Nevertheless, it was a terrific improvement to have a repeating rifle, and we were proud to be selected to use them.

The officers were called together after a major from headquarters arrived during the third week in January. The reason for his visit was the reorganization of our regiment. In April, a muster-out of the regiment comprising the Reserve Corps would occur. The major wanted figures on how many of the original three year men would be leaving. A large number of veterans and recruits whose time had not expired would still be on hand. The major hoped to encourage as many men as possible to re-enlist, but he knew three years had been enough for most soldiers.

The results of the survey were that two new regiments would be formed composed of veteran volunteers and recent recruits. The regiments would be the 190th and the 191st. I would be in he 190th with my buddies Cliff and Alex, and the regiment would be commanded by Col. Hartshorne. We would still be part of the Fifth Corps, Army of The Potomac. As veteran volunteers Cliff, Alex, and I were among those offered the opportunity to re-enlist as army "teamsters," driving supply and medical wagons. We were given a day to think it over. It was a serious decision to make.

We sat around the fireplace in our hut that evening and discussed the offer. I explained my feelings. "Alex, unless you have ideas to the contrary, why don't you muster out? You'll have served your three years soon, and you can marry Carolyn and get started on a civilian job and live happily ever after! There will be plenty of work as long as the war continues, and you'll have a head start on the rest of us.

Cliff agreed and said, "Yes sir, if I had a pretty girl on the string like you do, I'd call it quits and go home. It sure wouldn't be any disgrace. You've fought as hard as anyone and come closer to being killed than most of us. Of course you'd sure miss us, but you'd get over it in time."

Alex was stretched out on his bunk with his hands under his head looking at the ceiling. He turned to us and said, "I knew our enlistment would be up in a few weeks, and I've been thinking about it for a good while, especially since Carolyn said she'd marry me. Her father has offered me a job in a small plant he runs in Williamsport. In peacetime, they make metal goods like cookware, eating utensils, buckets, and so on. Right now,

Drifting To Glory

they're covered up with work due to the war, and I'd have no trouble earning a living.

I can tell you I'm tired of this damned army life – all the buffoons and sons-of-bitches who tell us what to do. Hell, the majority of 'em aren't smart enough to pour piss out of a boot! I've enjoyed just about as much of this foolishness as I care to, and agree with what you've just said. I'm gonna turn in that new Spencer and call it a day."

Alex hopped out of his bunk, looked at us, and smiled. He knew we'd be happy for him. Cliff and I slapped him on his back and congratulated him on his wise decision.

"Well, one smart fella out of three ain't bad," I said. "Of course that drops us down to "Two Musketeers," but it'll have to do. Cliff and I are going to see this war through or die trying...beg your pardon...poor choice of words."

"I knew you two were long term sufferers," Alex said. "You'll probably both become officers like McNew, and spend the rest of your lives riding herd on some poor, rear rank privates. I can picture gold epaulets on your coats, now."

"Fat chance of that," Cliff laughed.

"Yeah, like when hell freezes over," I added. "We came in as privates, and I have the feeling we'll go out the same."

We were really happy about Alex's choice to leave the army and knew we'd miss him. We weren't any happier than Alex. He smiled and joked all the way to the sutler's shop. We couldn't find any dime novels we hadn't read, so we bought some hard candy and went back to our home away from home.

The sky turned dark. A miserable, freezing rain began to fall. We added wood to our stove and got comfortable for the evening. We wrote letters telling our folks and friends about Alex's decision. I knew my folks would wonder why I opted to stay in until we won the war, but I wrote that I couldn't see giving up when we were almost at the gates of victory. They knew I wouldn't be the only one who felt the same way. We knew we'd be going home for good in 1864.

The next day Cliff and I spoke to the company commander. We told him it was our choice to re-enlist in the 190th Regt. as teamsters, rather than continue as infantry. He thought we'd made a good choice. The job was desirable to most men. Riding instead of marching with a heavy rifle

Drifting To Glory

and pack was an advancement as far as we could see. Also, we figured we had done our share as foot soldiers over almost three years of warfare. We'd let some fresh new fish take our places.

The regimental supply trains stayed behind the troops and carried or hauled everything the men could not carry on their backs. We joked that we might even eat better since we would be back closer to the herds of cattle that were driven behind the regiments. We liked the idea of being able to keep our Spencer carbines. Supply trains were often attacked by enemy cavalry, and the job could be "hazardous to our health," as Cliff put it.

So, on February 1, 1864, Cliff and I signed enlistment papers "to serve as teamsters in the Army of The United States of America for a period of three years, unless sooner discharged by proper authority." At the bottom of my enlistment form it read as follows:

> "I certify, on honor, That I have minutely inspected the above named volunteer, L. B. Danforth previously to enlistment, and that he was entirely sober when enlisted; and that, to the best of my judgement and belief, he is of lawful age, and that, in accepting him as duly qualified to perform the duties of an able-bodied soldier, I have strictly observed the Regulations which govern the recruiting service. This soldier has blue eyes, brown hair, fair complexion, is five feet eleven inches high."
>
> ROGER SHERMAN
> First Regt. of Rifles P.R.V.C. Volunteers
> Adjutant - Recruiting Officer

We were signed up for another three years, but that didn't really bother us as we knew damned well the war would be over in a matter of months. We thought we had made a smart move, especially when many others were turned down for the work.

Alex was now a civilian. We thought it only proper that he should have a farewell party, and since he would be passing through Washington on his way home, we put in for a weekend pass to Washington. We were among the "elite," that is, Veteran Volunteers, and had no problem in obtaining the passes. It was our only chance to celebrate Alex's discharge before he left, so a happy mood prevailed among the old "Three Musketeers." We got transportation easily enough as well established trips had been set up between the camps and the capital. The distance was fairly short and the routes were now constantly protected by Union cavalry.

Washington continued to be a busy city. The capitol building stood majestically on the horizon. The capitol dome had just been finished in 1863, and this was the first opportunity for us to see it up close during daylight. It was a beautiful sight with the white dome shining in the sunlight.

Alex stared at it for a minute, and exclaimed, "Wouldn't it be a terrible disgrace if Rebel artillery ever got close enough to drop some shells on that beautiful building?" He added quickly, "I'm relying on you elite veterans to see that it never happens."

"Your wish is our command, oh illustrious private citizen!"

"By, you sound like a poet," Cliff said.

"It's odd you should say that, Cliff, because my first name really is 'Lord.' My mother's name was Mary Lord, and they named me Lord Byron Danforth, using her maiden name. Heck, my pay chits show 'L. Byron Danforth' most of the time, but once in a while they show up as 'Byron L. Danforth'. I'd hate to think they might get so confused that they'd start paying me twice each payday. Maybe I could put on a fake beard and go through the pay line a second time."

"I think you're both beginning to show definite signs of battle nostalgia, and maybe the army has done the wrong thing in allowing you to re-enlist," Alex said. "I'll accept you both, though, weird or not. Let's go eat. I'm starved."

We enjoyed a tasty meal at one of the hotel restaurants. The beef we ate did not bear much resemblance to what we ate in the army. We decided the civilians had access to a better grade of beef cattle, or could it be better cooks? The bread was certainly better than weevil infested hard tack, too!

We were able to stay at the same hotel where we ate. It was a little removed from the main stream, fancier hotels, and our uniforms helped to secure a reduced rate. The hotel clerk was a disabled veteran with only one leg.

Before turning in for the night, we visited the hotel saloon and toasted Alex's entry into civilian life. We talked about the times we had endured, both good and bad. It was not easy saying good night. We sat on the hotel veranda and said little, smoking cigars in the dim light of a gas lamp, watching a light rain fall.

In the morning, Alex was anxious to start home, so after our one night on the town, we walked to the train station. Alex got his ticket and we strolled out to the coach. Alex said, "I don't want to drag this farewell out and run the chance of you guys crying over my departure, so I'll just say good-bye for now. I can't tell you how great it has been soldiering with you and hope we can get together again, soon. Please do your damndest to keep from dying of lead poisoning! There's nothing like dying in bed of old age or becoming overly excited with some good gal rolling around in the hay."

"You've quite a knack for saying the nicest things," Cliff said, laughing.

"Seriously, Al, this war should be over this year," I said, "if Uncle Abe can just get his hands on a general who'll take the bull by the horns and get the job done. God knows from the acres of cannon and equipment we saw outside of the capital, we must have the hardware to finish the job!"

Alex hugged us and climbed aboard the train. In spite of what he's said, kidding us about tears, he couldn't help a few from starting down his cheeks.

"Give Carolyn our regards," we hollered as Alex waved. We watched sadly and waved back as the train chugged out of the station. I was glad to see the smoke and steam obscure his departure.

Cliff said, "By, I feel like a little something to drink – something like 'spirits' to lift my spirits, so to speak. What do you say?"

"I'll drink to that," I replied, wiping my eyes. As we crossed the street and opened the door to the tavern, several young soldiers exited, laughing and singing. They started to chant, "In eighteen hundred and sixty four, we'll all go home and fight no more!"

I smiled sadly and looked at Cliff, saying, "God, I sure hope they know what they're chanting about."

Chapter XVI

We read in the paper during February that the U.S. Congress had reinstated the old grade of Lieutenant General, and in March, President Lincoln nominated Gen. Grant for that rank. The Senate promptly confirmed the nomination, and the President named Grant as General-in-Chief of the Army of the United States. The President believed he had finally found the man who could lead the armies to victory. Grant came east leaving Gen. Sherman in command in the western theater.

Gen. Grant took command of the Army of The Potomac at its headquarters in Brandy Station, Va. Gen. Meade would still command the army under Grant and would begin a close working relationship with him. Grant made preparation for advancing all the armies, east and west, simultaneously, and instructed Meade to follow Lee's army wherever it moved.

By late April of '64, spring weather had improved to the point where the army could move ahead. We had begun our new duties as regimental teamsters with the ammunition train, following closely behind the troops. This was new duty for us and we liked the change of routine.

We drove the standard army supply wagon with a two-team set of mules. The mules were preferred to horses as they could handle rougher terrain better; could get by on poorer food; and could stand harsher treatment. When the roads were very wet and full of ruts, three teams were often used, especially when the loads were very heavy.

Unlike the stagecoach and ambulance wagons, the teamster did not ride on the wagon, but on the "near pole" mule; that is, the first mule to the left in front of the wagon. A saddle was provided on this mule. The driver used a single rein connected to the "near leader" mule, also on the left at the front, and from his collar, an iron rod fastened to the bit of the "off leader." A line was provided back to the brake of the left rear wheel. It was a good working arrangement. We used the regular commands of "Gee," "Haw," and "Yay." We frequently used other stronger words that were probably wasted on the mules, but made us feel better!

The wagons were ten feet long and usually had the insignia of the unit on the canvas; in our case, the blue Maltese cross of the Fifth Corps. The type of contents was normally stencilled on the canvas, too, such as "ordnance." The ammunition wagons had precedence over all other supply wagons. A standard number of wagons would be about twenty-five for each one thousand men. It was not unusual to have five thousand wagons supporting an army. Loaded wagons enroute to the front, and empty wagons returning, could cause some huge traffic jams, especially when troops and artillery had priority.

Most wagons we used for supplies had no springs, unlike the medical ambulances, which had a crude spring arrangement. Unfortunately, many wounded men were transported in any type wagon available, especially in the early years of the war. They suffered an agonizing trip, jostled over rough, country roads. During heavy rains, the wounded often became drenched due to leaking canvas, and sometimes had no covering at all. They were transferred to rail or boat transport when possible.

In early May, Grant hoped to cut off Lee's army from Richmond by attacking across the Wilderness – an area of dense forest and underbrush about fifteen miles wide, east to west, and ten miles, north to south. Infantry had difficulty moving through a jungle of trees, vines, briars, and thorn bushes. Our wagon trains were confined to the few roads entering the area. It was a terrible place to try to fight a major battle. The commanders on both sides had problems trying to maneuver their units into position. Sporadic fights broke out in the woods, setting dead leaves and underbrush on fire, causing thick smoke. Most unit commanders on both sides had problems determining where the enemy was located.

The fires increased in intensity. Many wounded men could not get help and burned to death in the woods. The fighting stopped at times when the men of both sides agreed to try to save their wounded.

What had started out to be a grand attack by Grant's army ended in a tangle of disorganized brigades and halted wagon trains. Grant's casualties were in excess of seventeen thousand after three days of fighting. The Confederates lost less than half that number.

The battle ended as a draw similar to others in the past, and our Union forces moved toward the town of Spotsylvania.

While our men were engaged in the Wilderness, the Bucktail regimen-

Drifting To Glory

tal wagon train was strung out in the rear of the regiment. Supplies had been moved forward on the backs of men and mules. It was very hot and humid, and we were lolling about waiting for orders when we were attacked by a force of fifty or more Confederate cavalry. Cliff and I grabbed our carbines and ducked under the wagons. Holes were already showing up in the canvas tops. We could see the other teamsters taking cover, too. Our mules jostled about a little, but they were battle hardened and stood their ground.

I fired at one of the gray troopers nearest to me, and knew I had hit him, but he remained in the saddle and rode off. As the troops rode on down the line of wagons, I shouted to Cliff, "I thought we'd be out of infantry duty in this work, but I'm about to dig a trench and crawl in it."

Cliff reloaded his Spencer and hollered, "Hell, By, we'll be able to tell our grandkids someday that we fought right where the bullets were the thickest – underneath the ammunition wagon!"

I almost laughed, but stopped abruptly as bullets started flicking up dirt around me and making whacking noises in the canvas. The enemy riders circled back for another pass at us and were taking their work very seriously. Evidently no one had told these superb horsemen that they were losing the war!

A cheer arose from our teamsters as we beheld the beautiful sight of our blue cavalry charging out of an adjoining section of woods and closing on the Rebel troopers. They were all out of sight in seconds, but we could hear the firing and the troops whooping and hollering in the distance.

We crawled from under the wagons and began to talk to the other teamsters. I said, "Boys, if we can count on this kind of protection on a regular basis, we won't have too much to worry about." A quick check revealed no casualties among the men, but several mules had been shot and one wagon was on fire. We drove our wagons quickly out of the area as the burning ammunition wagon exploded like a Fourth of July celebration.

We were happy to pick up mail back at our base depot while our wagons were being reloaded. I looked forward to the news from home and to the newspaper clippings mother usually included. I often learned more about the progress of the war from these clippings than I did from the news which circulated around camp. It seemed odd considering I was only a few miles from the scene of battle.

Mother wrote that she and the girls met with other ladies once a week at church. They rolled bandages and took them to the hospital at Olean where they were shipped to military hospitals.

It was comforting to read that Grant was making progress hammering away at Lee's entrenchments. The Wilderness fighting appeared to have been a draw, but the papers stated that Grant did things that the previous generals did not – he followed up a setback with a renewal of the offensive.

After the terrible fighting in May at Spotsylvania, North Anna, and at Cold Harbor, Grant had casualties of over 33,000 men. Some of those who criticized him called him "butcher Grant." But our men could be replaced. Even though the Confederacy had adopted conscription a year before we did, Lee was having serious problems finding replacements for his depleted regiments. Desertions were becoming a major problem on both sides, according to the newspapers, and the exchange of prisoners had been stopped by Grant. I could understand how some men finally got enough of the bloodshed and hardships and just walked away.

Our wagon trains continued to shuttle back and forth behind the lines of the battles in Virginia, bringing more of everything the army needed. Rebel cavalry became increasingly more proficient at raiding, capturing, or burning our wagon trains. They were able to seize armaments, foodstuffs, and medical supplies they could barely supply on their own, anymore.

We often spoke to prisoners as they were marched past us to the rear. One lanky Reb said, "We sure like those Spencer carbines you folks have. They make a different "popping" sound when they go off. We used some for about a week until we ran out of cartridges for them…could have killed a lot more of you 'blue bellies' if we'd had more of 'em. We like your food, too, and have been eating more of your food than ours."

I smiled at him, asking, "You've captured some wagons of those 'dessicated' vegetables, haven't you? You like those dried up vegetables?

"You mean those damned dried up weeds that ya add water to? They are so bad that we've started feeding the stuff to our mules, but then…you get hungry enough, they really don't taste so bad mixed up with corn meal mush or something. We call the hard tack 'worm castles' 'cause it gets infested with weevils and maggots. You eat 'em in the dark you can't tell the difference."

I laughed at him because I knew there was more truth than fiction in what he'd said. "Yep, Reb, I know just what you mean. We've got where we call those dried weeds, 'desecrated' vegetables." I tried to kid him a little and said, "I hear since our men don't like that dried up stuff they are going to start feeding all of it to you Rebel prisoners." I looked at him and laughed.

The Reb turned back as the line of prisoners walked away and remarked, "You Yankee privates eat as good or better than our officers, so anything we get in prison camp can't be all that bad. And by the way, Yank, we're all through being shot at, but you'd better keep an eye peeled. The next Reb cavalry trooper may be using one of those Spencer pop guns on you!"

"I'll be watching," I said. "You Rebs are good shots."

The ordnance train we were in lumbered around a bend in the road and started down a grade where we would cross the Totopotomoy Creek. The area was somewhat soggy, and the teamsters were having difficulty driving the wagons across. We got off our mules and stood in the shade of a tree while a teamster tried to get his teams moving. He had four big horses in harness on his rig, but they still weren't making any headway. The rough looking teamster started whipping his horses, and we couldn't believe it when he began to beat the lead horse in the head with the butt end of his whip. He started swearing, using some of the foulest language we had heard in quite a while.

Unbeknown to this rogue, a group of officers on horseback rode up to cross the creek in time to see the incident. The officers included Gen. Grant and several staff officers. When Grant saw what the teamster was doing and heard his swearing, he trotted over to him and hollered, "What do you think you are doing, you stupid ass? Quit beating those horses at once!"

The teamster looked at Grant without recognizing him and said, "Well, who are you to try to tell me how to do my job?"

Grant shook his fist at him and said, "I'm about to let you know who I am!" Grant loved horses and hated profanity and turned to an officer and said, "Have this human jackass tied to a tree for the remainder of the day as punishment for cruelty to animals. He's driven his last team in this army!"

I looked at Cliff. We stood there wide eyed as we witnessed the scene. We knew we would never forget it. I said, "I'll be feeding my teams extra grain starting tonight. There's no excuse for treating an animal like that."

Cliff said, "I'll bet you one thing, By. I believe that son-of-a-bitch will recognize Grant next time, if he ever sees him again. I also hope he has to wet his pants while he's tied to that tree."

"I wouldn't be surprised if he hasn't, already," I said.

Drifting To Glory

Chapter XVII

By July, our army had become stalemated at Petersburg, Va. A portion of the corps had fought up the peninsula from eastern Virginia. Many regiments moved up the James River on boats, pulling barges of equipment strung to behind them. This resulted in additional areas which had to be defended by the Confederates.

In spite of the fact that we were halted before Petersburg, Gen. Sheridan's regiments were pushing down the Shenandoah Valley. Gen. Sherman's army was slowly fighting in a southeast direction in northern Georgia. It was reported that Pres. Lincoln had said he knew the hole where Sherman burrowed in, but he wasn't too sure just where he'd come out. I read this encouraging information from a copy of the Olean Times Herald that mother had mailed to me.

Our Bucktails were fighting as part of the offensive against Lee's forces entrenched at Petersburg, Va. during the period from June through August. Repeated attempts failed to dislodge the Confederates, and the city had been under siege for months. Our forces attempted to breach their lines by mining beneath them. Soldiers who had been former coal miners dug below the entrenchments and detonated several tons of gun powder. The explosion killed many men and left a huge crater. The attack that followed failed and added to the Union casualties more than the Confederate.

To add to the Federal woes, Confederate Gen. Jubal Early made a serious threat against Washington by once more invading the north. He moved quickly, much like Stonewall Jackson's troops, and captured Hagerstown, Md. with little opposition. He crossed into Pennsylvania with cavalry forces and burned Chambersburg, Pa. when the town could not come up with $500,000 in cash, which he had demanded. Many of his men believed he could have captured Washington if Early had not broken off the attack. His troops had been on the outskirts of the city when they withdrew. I guess old "Jubal" had his reasons – he might have thought the city was too well defended, but he definitely threw a scare into the residents of the capital. Civilians had armed themselves, having no doubt they would have to take to the streets to defend themselves and their homes.

The Bucktail infantry advanced on the eighteenth of August and deployed in a position that left their flanks exposed and unprotected. The Rebels quickly took advantage of this tactical error, capturing a large portion of a brigade. These Bucktails were sent off to prison camps at Richmond and Danville, Va., and Salisbury, N.C. They would have rather taken their chances being shot at than confined as prisoners.

Cliff and I thought we had escaped danger, but we were surprised to see more gray cavalry right under the noses of our own forces. They were beginning to make a habit of showing up when least expected, and we did our best to defend ourselves once again. They were thick as flies and came thundering among the wagons, shooting and hollering like a bunch of renegades. They were the wildest bunch we had seen thus far. I saw the flash of a rifle only a few yards away, and that was the last thing I remembered.

Chapter XVIII

I awoke smelling disinfectant and urine. I could see a hazy, white mist around me which gradually focused into a white hospital ward. My head throbbed on the right side, and I felt thick bandages wrapped around my head above my eyes. I wondered how I had ended up here. I wiggled my toes and legs and found I could move everything that was supposed to move and assumed I was all in one piece. Only my head ached and I had a stiff neck. My thoughts returned to the wagon train. I wondered what had happened to Cliff.

I wondered where Alex was and suddenly realized he'd been discharged and gone home. My thinking was fuzzy. I remembered Ed Dodd and could still hear the explosion that killed him. The thought of the Three Musketeers came to mind, and it appeared that the three had been reduced to one – at least for the time being.

As these thoughts rolled over in my mind, I heard a voice say, "Well, Danforth, other than a splitting headache, how are we feeling this afternoon?"

I looked up to see a middle aged doctor looking at me over his spectacles and smiling as though we were old friends. I answered, "You're right about the headache, but other than a few jumbled thoughts, I guess I'm not too bad off. Suppose you tell me how I am and how I got here, sir."

"Well, private, all I know is that your chart tells me you arrived here with a wagon train of wounded on Tuesday P.M. It is now Thursday so you have had a nice two day snooze. As for your wound, you were shot in the head – just barely. The ball that hit you chiseled a neat little trench along the side of your noggin over your right ear. The Reb should become a sculptor – very good job. Had he been a bit more accurate, you would have three eye sockets, and you wouldn't be here to avail yourself of my services. Any other questions?"

"Yes, sir, I've a couple questions. What hospital is this, and what did you say your name is? Also, you said I've been here two days. Have you come across a patient named Pvt. Clifford Young in the last two days?"

"Excuse my poor manners," the doctor said. "We stay so busy around here, I sometimes forget who I am and what I'm doing. Yes, you've been asleep here two days, but there won't be any additional charge for the rest period. My name is Major Butcher and I'm one of the ward surgeons here at Mount Pleasant Hospital in Washington. I don't remember a Pvt. Young, but he could be here on another floor, perhaps. You can check with one of the admissions people about him."

"Thank you, sir," I said. "Excuse me, but did you say your name is Major Butcher, sir?"

The doctor smiled and looked over his glasses at me. "Yes, that's the name, and I know what you're thinking, son. I've heard quite a few comments about being a 'Major Butcher.' A 'Captain Butcher,' or 'Lt. Col. Butcher' would sound less grotesque, wouldn't it...especially if I'm assisting on a ward with amputations?"

I smiled and said, "I wish you a quick promotion to Lt. Col., sir."

"Thank you for the thought, private. You get all the bed rest you can. If you feel like sitting up on the side of the bed, that's fine, but don't go walking off to use the latrine. I put about fourteen stitches in your scalp, and I don't want you to move around more than necessary and possibly start your wound bleeding again. When you have to go, just use that 'thunder pot' under the bed. I'll see you when I make my rounds again in the morning. I want to keep an eye on you for a few days and make sure you're not acting strangely. Sometimes head wounds can affect your thinking, walking, or talking. You seem to be doing fine so far."

"Thanks for the advice, doc," I said. "I'm not planning any visits to town, and I'll try to act no stranger than usual." Major Butcher smiled and strolled on down the ward.

I stretched out in bed enjoying the rest. It had been a good while since I'd had the pleasure of sleeping between clean white sheets, and I wasn't in any real hurry to leave. I was concerned about what had happened to Cliff. I spoke to an admissions lady who came through the ward. Her name was Bonnie Maggard, and she returned later to inform me that she had no record of Cliff being admitted at this hospital. She said it could take several weeks to check with all the other hospitals. At this time, there were sixteen hospitals in the city of Washington with others in Alexandria, Va. and

Drifting To Glory

the surrounding area.

I made good progress and my fine doctor, Maj. Michael Butcher, estimated that I should be able to return to duty within two weeks. I spent the time reading, writing letters, and visiting with other convalescents. The amputees were all on one floor in several wards. I met Dr. Paul Ronca who was a specialist in that field. It sickened me to see so many amputees with stumps of arms and legs all bandaged. Some men who had been here for weeks were getting fitted for wooden or cork limbs.

Dr. Ronca explained the reason they had to remove so many limbs. He said, "As you know, a 'Minie' ball fired from a rifle is a pretty good chunk of lead, and when it strikes a bone it normally shatters or splinters the bone beyond any repair. There is no choice but to amputate."

The doctor told me of one case where a soldier would have been missed by a twelve pound solid shot, fired from a cannon. Balls often traveled slowly enough in the air to be seen with the naked eye. After hitting the ground a ball rolled across the field, and the soldier ran to it, thinking it was moving slowly enough that he could stop it with his foot. The cannon ball had sufficient muzzle energy remaining that it severed the soldier's foot at the ankle. The war was over for him.

I looked at crowded conditions and wished I could leave soon and give up my bed for someone who needed it much worse than I did.

I continued my medical education in my tours around the hospital wards. Some men had no visitors and were not hospitalized with anyone they knew. They were pleased to talk with anyone, if they could talk, and I enjoyed chatting with them and learning where they were from. I wrote letters for some men and occasionally helped the ward attendants and the nurses – both male and female. Any help was appreciated.

Most wards had windows all the way around and blinds that could be opened to allow sunshine and a flow of fresh air through the ward. This helped to alleviate the odors of rotting flesh, human excrement, dressings that were overdue for changing, and the disinfectant that sometimes became overpowering.

A large ward on one floor contained those men who had contracted a venereal disease. Most soldiers took no precautions when engaging in "horizontal refreshments." I learned from the doctors on that ward that rubber "sheaths" had come into use after the process of vulcanization of rubber was invented in 1844. The sheaths were fairly expensive, and most men were embarrassed to purchase them until the diseases became more widespread, and even then, some soldiers complained that using the sheaths was like taking a shower with your raincoat on. I was interested to note that many men didn't care if they got a venereal disease since it often meant a ticket home if they weren't cured in a reasonable length of time by the army physician.

Treating the disease was not a quick nor easy process. It normally consisted of a combination of hope and guesswork. The doctors experimented with various treatments such as the use of silver nitrate, mercury, pokeweed, elderberries, and silkweed root in whiskey. Sometimes, pills of resin from pine trees was used. Nothing was proclaimed as a sure cure.

One doctor treated a Rebel soldier for a broken leg who reported being in a venereal disease ward in a Richmond hospital. He seemed to be cured of the disease. He told the story that the Richmond Hospital was right across the street from a house of prostitution. The girls advertised by exposing themselves at their windows, and many of the patients who could walk were found absent from their beds at bed check and could have been located in beds across the street.

Dr. Butcher finally pronounced me in good enough health to be returned to service after three weeks at the hospital. I had mixed emotions about leaving, but knew I had to go back to my duty. Unfortunately, Mrs. Maggard advised me that the result of the checks she had made with other hospitals had not turned up anything on Cliff's whereabouts. I bid Dr. Butcher good-bye and thanked him for all his help and kindness. I also wished the best for my other friends I had met during my short stay at Mount Pleasant Hospital.

Chapter XIX

Upon return to my base of operations, I attempted to learn what had happened to Cliff. The officer I spoke with told me a number of wagons and teamsters had been captured, and he was unable to tell me more. I was saddened that Cliff had evidently been taken prisoner. I hoped he had not been wounded and thought I might be able to find out more accurate information later.

The men remaining in the Bucktail regiments were bivouacked east of Petersburg, fighting as skirmishers again. Those who had escaped capture were transferred to the 2nd Division of the Fifth Corps under the command of Gen. Ayers. I had returned from the hospital in September and now drove my wagon in a train supporting this division.

Our main supply base was at City Point, Va. on the James River. Enormous amounts of supplies moved up the James River from the Norfolk area to that point. Our wagons were loaded here and moved south and west to supply the army.

The fall of 1864 dragged on with little progress against Lee's forces. The men of both sides dug trenches, and the movement stagnated around the Petersburg area. Occasionally, regiments would be called upon to adjust their positions in an effort to probe for a weakness in the enemy lines. The summer and fall had been so dry that any movements were immediately signalled by a rising cloud of dust from hundreds of marching feet.

Confederate cavalry were not only skilled at capturing wagon trains. During the siege at Petersburg, Rebel cavalry captured several hundred head of Union army beef cattle, which were well received by Lee's hungry troops.

By November of 1864, it was apparent that the war would not be won by the end of the year, in spite of the fact that great progress had been made. Gen. Sherman, after taking Atlanta, had embarked on a march to the sea, capturing Savannah, Ga. He presented it to President Lincoln as a Christmas "gift." Also in December, in Tennessee, Gen. Hood's Army of Tennessee was reduced to an ineffective force after being defeated by Union Gen. Thomas at Franklin and Nashville. The newspapers in the north covered these victories in a widespread fashion. Everyone was encouraged and had reason to celebrate the holiday season.

Petersburg, Va. was still under siege at the end of 1864, and Richmond remained in Confederate hands. The armies once again ceased most of their operations and prepared to enter their winter camps.

The U. S. Navy had been successful in blockading southern ports and was able to continue their work at sea throughout the winter months. We learned after the fall of Mobile in August, only Wilmington, N.C. remained available to the south for blockade running.

The President and the country were disappointed that the war would extend into 1865, but all the indications pointed to a Union victory before many months would pass.

It was on this basis that I decided not to try to go home for Christmas. I was convinced the war would really end in the early spring, and I'd be heading home for good by that time.

During the second week of December, I received a letter from a soldier who was confined in a prison camp with Cliff in Salisbury, N.C. Cliff had been too weak to write and had asked his fellow captive, Bill Foote, to write for him. Foote was from a little settlement near Ceres named Shinglehouse, Pa. He was from Co. K of the Bucktails.

In the letter Cliff had indicated that he was doing pretty good with the little food they were getting and that the weather was very cold. He also wrote he knew I had been shot in the head, and the Rebels had left me for dead.

Mother wrote a note which Mrs. Young included with her letter to Cliff. She told Cliff I was alive and had recovered from my wound. I wrote to Cliff, too, and hoped my letter would reach him. I wondered if he had been wounded, but had not written about it to keep from worrying his parents.

I hated the thought of Cliff suffering in a prison camp. We had been through some close calls together for three years, and I was afraid he'd be confined for the remainder of the war unless we liberated the camp before then.

I was depressed over the news about Cliff, but still didn't want to go home as Christmas approached. I knew I needed to get away from camp, at least for a while, and got a five day furlough. I decided to go to Washington and thought I'd try to locate Lt. Preble, if he was still stationed at the War Department. I remembered his sisters, too, and had pleasant thoughts of possibly seeing them again.

Christmas in the capital had not changed much since our 1862 visit. If anything, it was more brightly decorated for the holidays. Lines of festooned decorations were draped across the streets, and each gas lamppost had a wreath hanging below the lamp. Red, green, and silver ribbons stretched across the store fronts. Union flags were displayed everywhere.

It had not snowed recently, but the temperature was below freezing. There were dirty piles of old snow along the streets and on the corners, leftover from the last blizzard. A bright sun reflected off the decorations in the streets and on the stores. White billowing clouds were sailing on a sharp northwest wind, and I had the feeling a new snowfall was on the way.

I made inquiries of Lt. Preble at the War Department and was shunted from office to office until I located him. His office had a shiny new spittoon by the door, and I noticed that several tobacco chewers had missed their target.

He was now Captain Preble, and smiled at me saying, "Great to see you again, Byron. Believe it's been two years. How have you been, and how are your buddies? Evidently you've all been doing your part to win the war. We've done pretty good this year – too bad we couldn't have wrapped it up before '65.

"Congratulations on your promotion, captain," I said as I saluted. I brought him up to date on our activities. He was pleased that Alex had not been more seriously wounded and had decided not to re-enlist. He was sorry to hear of Cliff's capture.

Changing the subject, he asked, "How long are you going to be in the city? I want you to stay with us as long as you can, and I promise you won't have to sleep in a stable this time! We've finished an addition to the house and have two more bedrooms now. My parents and the girls will be happy to see you again. Lee is recently engaged, but Mary is still unattached. You can even have a bedroom right next to Mary's. I'll tell her you put in a special request for it."

"Captain, you're determined to try to get me in trouble."

"You'll be in trouble if you don't quit calling me captain. My name's

Drifting To Glory

Dave, remember? And I'll call you By."

"That's fine, but I don't want to impose on you, again."

"Nonsense – we don't have company this year. Most of our friends are from out of town and have gone home for the holidays. Let's go get some lunch, and I can wind things up here for the week. It's Friday and Christmas is Sunday so you can at least spend the weekend with us."

I noticed the lieutenant had been seated while we talked, and his left arm was in his lap. He stood up to get his hat, and I saw that he had lost his left hand. I was stunned but said nothing.

"I see you've noticed my slight disability," David said. "Let me tell you how that came about while we eat lunch." We sat at a table by a window, watching the last minute Christmas shoppers hurrying by. It had started to snow.

"I could have spent the rest of the war sitting at that desk," he said, "but after Fredericksburg the 'cause' got to me, I guess, and I had to get into the war for real. I joined a Maryland artillery outfit and trained with them. I lost my hand at Chancellorsville, fighting with Gen. Hooker's troops. When I got out of the hospital, the War Department was kind enough to take me back, especially since I was right handed and could still scribble out the paperwork they needed. Of course, it could have been worse…could have lost the arm."

"By the way, I've noticed that area over your ear where the hair doesn't quite cover. Was your last haircut a saber cut?" He laughed and I had to laugh with him at his pun.

"No," I answered, "some gray horse soldier didn't like the way I wore my hair and just rifled a new part in it for me! I wear my kepi a little low on that side of my head so it hardly shows. I'm very sorry about your hand. It was a dear price to pay."

"Oh, I get along pretty well," David admitted, "and they think they can work out some kind of artificial rubber hand for me, although I think the old hook they've used for years might be more useful. I guess I could try them both."

We finished lunch and walked to the livery stable to get David's horse. "We're a little short of horses since so many men have already left for the holidays, so just mount up behind me and we'll head home. This big bay brute can carry us both without even knowing it." The horse's warm breath formed miniature clouds as he puffed through the freezing air.

Drifting To Glory

No one was at David's home when we arrived, but shortly thereafter Mary walked up on the porch, arms full of packages. I opened the door for her, and she looked surprised and very pretty, with rosy cheeks and snow covered clothes.

"Well, merry Christmas to you Byron! I thought you'd never come back to see us again. I'm so glad you did." She put the packages on the hall table, hurried over to me, and gave me a big hug, saying, "Please excuse my snowy clothes. Now I see I'll have one last gift to get for someone."

"I'm happy to see you again, Mary," I said as I helped her remove her coat and overshoes.

"If I had any more snow on me, you'd have to sweep me off with a broom on the front porch, By. Mother used to do that task for Lee and me," Mary said, smiling.

"You look pretty as a painting with snow flakes in your black hair and rosy cheeks, too," I said.

"My, you're so very charming, Private Danforth. The army hasn't ruined you completely, have they? They didn't do much for poor David, I'm sorry to say." She looked at David with a sorrowful expression.

David was sitting on the davenport, smoking his pipe, observing our little meeting, and spoke up, saying, "By, as you may have remembered from your last visit, my 'old' sisters have always watched over their little brother like a couple of mother hens. I keep telling them to behave and be thankful they still have ninety-five percent of me to boss around."

Mr. and Mrs. Preble and Lee and her fiancee arrived. Our supper had been prepared by their cook, and we enjoyed a hearty winter meal of roast beef, potatoes, and green vegetables. The vegetables reminded me of our desiccated vegetables, and I wondered if they had found their way onto civilian tables? I thought it best not to mention it.

Lee's beau, Donald Morris, was studying to be a doctor and had been getting some on the job experience at Carver Hospital in Washington. I discovered he was quite familiar with the types of wounds that soldiers received. After supper, he told me my wound appeared to have healed very well. He thought my hair would grow in to cover most of the scar. I told him I no longer had any headaches except for the one we all had, knowing that the war would not end in 1864.

When asked about the whereabouts of Cliff and Alex, I told my friends about Alex returning to civilian life and about Cliff's capture and imprisonment. Everyone expressed the hope that Cliff would not have to remain a prisoner much longer. We discussed the disadvantages of the cessation of prisoner exchanges. It seemed much harder on imprisoned men, even though able-bodied men usually returned to the ranks when they were exchanged. Grant believed this prolonged the war for everyone, and the federal government backed him up.

Mary took me on a buggy tour of the government buildings on Saturday. The offices were closed for the holidays, but I enjoyed seeing the main buildings and climbing the steps of the capitol. I told Mary what Alex had said about keeping the beautiful capitol building safe from harm.

The snow had continued to fall and it turned bitterly cold. We were pleased to return to the warmth of the house, after stopping at a store to purchase a Christmas gift.

On Christmas eve, we opened gifts around a large hemlock tree which the girls had decorated. Mary gave me new leather gloves and a scarf, which would be very useful. I gave her a scarf, too, and a bottle of perfume, which I believe she saw me purchase where we had shopped.

Everyone attended a church service on Christmas morning not far from the house. The snow had stopped falling, but the day was gray and very cold. We were happy to spend the day indoors around the large brick fireplace in the living room. Lee and Mary took turns playing the piano, and we enjoyed singing carols and patriotic songs.

I had to be back in camp on Tuesday, so we made the most of Monday. Mary and I went for a long walk and tried out our new scarves. After a period of silence she asked me, "By, what are your plans when the war is over? I know you'll want to go home to see your family, but then what will you do?"

I was quick to answer. "I really don't know what I want to do after that. I've seen so many places and done nothing but soldiering that I'm not sure I can settle down working at my father's inn, again. I guess I'll have to think about it and just cross that bridge when I get to it. I know I'm not the same person I was when I went off to war."

"I'm sure you're not," she answered. "I've noticed a change in you since you visited with us the last time. You seem more serious and a little distant…a result of the war, I imagine." I looked at her and smiled, but had no response for what she had said. She added, "If you have the chance to visit with us again, I'll do my best to take your mind off the war, By."

Drifting To Glory

"You've helped to do that quite a bit over the last few days," I said, "and I'm thankful I found you at home and still unattached."

"Oh, I'm not an old maid just yet. I'm still young...only twenty-three, so we both have our lives ahead of us. Please be very careful and take good care of yourself so you'll be able to look back on these years with fond memories, if that's possible."

That night we all talked and told stories around the fire. We drank cocoa and snacked on cookies. Mr. Preble had stronger beverages available, too...Christmas cheer, he said.

Mary and I lingered until late, snuggled up next to the fire, after Lee's beau had departed and their parents had retired. We hated to see the evening end, knowing that I must leave in the morning. At bedtime, we climbed the stairs together, stopped by her door, and chatted in hushed tones. I kissed her good-night, and she said, "Don't get any ideas about getting up early, and running off without telling me good-bye, or I'll never forgive you!"

"Mary, I wouldn't dare leave without eating some of that excellent breakfast your cook serves."

She giggled and said, "Oh, it's the breakfast and not me that you don't want to miss. You're terrible and I don't know why I put up with you...good night, By."

In the morning after breakfast, we walked slowly to the staging area where army wagons departed for the various camps. Before I knew it, I had kissed her good-bye and left her with the promise that I would write often and return when I could.

It was a long, sad, cold trip back to camp, but at least this time I didn't have to walk half way.

Drifting To Glory

Chapter XX

I checked in at our huge supply base at City Point, Va. to pick up a new wagon and teams of mules. The winter operations of any size had concluded with Gen. Hood's defeat at Nashville, Tn. by Gen. Thomas in mid December. Gen. Grant had been critical of the delay in Gen. Thomas getting his army to move, but this was a perfect example of why most winter operations ceased until spring. An ice storm had occurred in the Nashville area. Horses, mules, and men could hardly remain on their feet, let alone move artillery and supply wagons. Gen. Grant had been on the verge of relieving Thomas when a thaw in the weather permitted operations to move forward. We were proud of the accomplishments of the Army of The Cumberland and enjoyed reading of their exploits in the newspapers. We were anxious to read of the spring accomplishments of the Army of The Potomac and hoped they would occur soon, ending with final victory.

As 1865 got underway, we began to haul new human "freight" in addition to our standard army goods. The army medical department had increased the influence it had sorely lacked in the early years of the conflict. At regimental, brigade, and division hospitals, the orderlies were usually men who were recovering from minor wounds or others detailed to the hospitals to do the work of nurses. Most nurses in city hospitals were men. Now, women were being used at a growing rate, and we delivered them to the hospitals behind the front lines. Our men were grateful to see them as most women were more compassionate, cleaner in appearance, and better trained at their work. I enjoyed talking with them on numerous long, bumpy rides to the field hospitals.

Another duty that we teamsters found repulsive was the hauling of dead bodies to the base at City Point. The area was becoming a large Union cemetery. Fortunately, we didn't have to bury the dead since other soldiers were detailed to that duty. When the ground was frozen, the bodies were stacked in rows and covered with canvas. Usually the ground was frozen only a few inches deep, and with pickaxes the job could be done without many days delay. Temporary grave markers were erected for those bodies that could be identified, but there were hundreds of others that were marked "unknown." Many men made their own identification tags so their bodies could at least have a name on the gravestone marker. Relatives could claim them later for reburial in their home cemeteries if desired.

In the south, where the weather presented fewer problems, except for heavy rains, Sherman's army had rested and resupplied at Savannah, Ga. We learned they were on the move again, this time moving north into the Carolinas. The aim was to link up with Grant's forces in Virginia to end the war.

"Uncle Billy," as Sherman's troops referred to him, kept up his path of destruction, fighting his way to Fayetteville, N.C. He fought one last battle at Bentonville, N.C.

One of the other teamsters whose wagon was frequently close to mine was Billy Walsh. When we learned about Sherman's campaign, I said, "Billy, if we had been attached to Sherman's army, we would have worn out several wagons and mules by this time. Can you imagine the miles his infantry walked from Atlanta to Savannah? No wonder they rested for a month. I bet there's very few fat guys in his ranks. Don't you know they had to bring in a whole shipload of shoes for them when they finally got to Savannah?"

Billy agreed and said, "I'll bet you something else, By. I'll bet by the time Sherman's boys left Savannah, there were a bunch of southern prostitutes who became rich ladies of the night!"

"I won't bet against you on that, Billy, and I'll also bet the Savannah bankers were just tickled to death to see those gals walk in and deposit those greenbacks and gold."

On March twenty-sixth, we noticed considerable activity at City Point. The rumors we had heard were confirmed the next day. President Lincoln, Generals Grant and Sherman, and Admiral Porter met to confer regarding the conclusion of the war. Everyone knew the end was near.

By the second of April, Petersburg was finally evacuated. The next day Richmond fell to overwhelming Union forces. We were betting on what day the war would end, but we also remembered how elusive Gen. Lee had been. We worried that he would somehow link up with Gen. Joe Johnston's army and fight on into the summer. The Rebels were starving and had lit-

Drifting To Glory

tle left to fight with; plus, their numbers were rapidly dwindling due to widespread desertions. Everyone was surprised at how quickly the end came, with Lee surrendering on April ninth. Grant's generous terms allowed the Confederates to keep their horses and mules, which he knew they would need for spring plowing. The officers were also allowed to keep their sidearms. We issued wagon loads of rations to Rebel troops, many of whom hadn't eaten in several days.

President Lincoln was relieved to see the end of hostilities at last. He quickly halted the draft and reduced requisitions for war materials. He had lived to see the end of the war, but not by much, as his assassination came on April fourteenth. He died the next morning, and the entire nation mourned. It was hard for us to believe he was gone. He had been our Commander-In-Chief for four long years. All the military posts were in a state of disbelief.

A few days after the surrender, Federal troops had driven through western North Carolina and had freed the captured Bucktails and other prisoners. We got information about their emaciated condition, and I was dismayed to learn that Cliff had not survived. He had been wounded and might have recovered if he had received proper treatment, but gangrene had developed in his wounded leg. He had died just a week or so before our troops liberated the camp. One of the other prisoners believed Cliff had developed pneumonia, too, and had written Cliff's parents about his passing. I knew I'd have Cliff in my thoughts for a long time.

Gen. Sherman accepted the surrender of Gen. Johnston's Confederates near Durham Station, N.C. on April fourteenth, and the main hostilities ended. Some minor fighting continued in the west until the summer of 1865. Some major celebrating continued in the east until the end of the year!

Our wagon trains were now busy hauling not only Federal war goods back from the war zones, but captured Confederate arms as well. Union cavalry with little else to do accompanied the wagon trains. There were still bands of marauders in the form of deserters and skulkers, both Union and Rebel, and the cavalry kept a lookout for these renegades. Wagons were being pilfered and teamsters killed.

A cavalry captain rode up next to my wagon and engaged me in conversation, introducing himself as Darrell Maggard from a Pennsylvania regiment. I said, "I think I've heard that name before." After pausing for a moment, I added, "I believe I have met your wife."

The captain raised his eyebrows in surprise and said, "Oh, how did that come about?"

I asked him, "Does she by any chance work at the Mount Pleasant Hospital in Washington?"

"Well, yes she does. I guess you have met her. The world keeps getting smaller, doesn't it?" the captain said.

I recounted my hospital experience and told him how his wife had tried to locate Cliff for me. He said, "I'm glad she was doing something of a constructive nature." He bid me good day and rode on down the line of wagons.

With the war at an end, it took time to gradually release the thousands of troops. Few agreed to spend any longer in the army than they had to. We had completed the duty for which we had come to the colors for our country, and now it was time to go home.

There was one last march that was required and we all proudly participated. A Grand Review of the armies was requested. It took two days for all of the armies to march down Pennsylvania Avenue past the reviewing stands. President Johnson, the generals, Secretary of War Stanton, Secretary of State Seward, and other government officials were in the main reviewing stands. Thousands of people lined the streets, and flowers and banners were everywhere. The officers' horses could hardly see due to the flower garlands hung around their necks. The surviving Bucktails marched with the Army of The Potomac, and I was with them. I had to admit I was a little out of practice when it came to marching, but I was so happy to be part of the whole shebang that I would have crawled down Pennsylvania Avenue just to be with the others.

The next day, on May twenty-fourth, the western armies of the Ohio, the Tennessee, and the Cumberland marched. These were Sherman's boys, and their uniforms were well worn and not as trim as those of The Army of The Potomac, but they received as much applause as any of the other units. Gen. Sherman was on horseback, leading his armies of lean, bronzed men with great pride. As on the day before, people watched from the streets, the windows of buildings, and on the roofs.

It had been a long war. Many regular troops and some volunteers were posted throughout the south as occupation troops. Most of them were not welcome, but they did help to keep the peace. I was pleased that I would not be around to draw any of that duty.

I told my friend, Billy Walsh, "Just think, it was only going to take a few months to beat the Rebels, and it ended up taking four years!"

Billy said, "Yeah, can you imagine how long it could have taken if the British had thrown in with the Rebels in a big way? We probably would have had to fight them again, too!"

We were in a good mood and happy to have it all behind us once and for all. The regimental officers told us we could get a physical exam before we left the ranks, and I said, "I might go by and let them take my temperature – they were pretty good to me in the hospital, but to be truthful, if I never see another 'sawbones' again as long as I live, I'll be quite content." My friends agreed.

The next morning in our camp outside of Washington, a notice was posted on the bulletin board. It outlined that the Federal government would be recruiting volunteers from the veteran ranks for a yet to be determined period of time. The work would involve exhuming, transporting, and reburial of the remains of the dead – both north and south, and the establishment of some national cemeteries. It would also require the rebuilding of private fences and some buildings destroyed by military action, and the general cleaning up of battlefield areas which had been ravaged by marching armies. Payment would be two dollars a day, payable monthly. Application could be made with commanding officers, and those interested should apply at once.

I read the notice and thought about the last time I had "applied at once." That work had lasted longer than I wanted.

Most men laughed at the offer, and one old veteran said, "Fat chance they'll get men to stay on and take a second look at all the carnage. I've got a feeling most men will be high tailing it for home as soon as someone says 'go'."

Billy asked, "Going home right away ain't you, By?"

"Oh yeah," I said. "I owe it to myself and my folks to go home for a while, but I've got to visit a friend here before I leave. Give me your address before you go, and I'll look you up in Potter County when I get home."

I hurried into the capital that afternoon to see Mary. The streets were still crowded with enthusiastic citizens and soldiers. They were beginning a long lasting celebration.

Drifting To Glory

We sat on the back porch swing and watched the birds splashing in the bird bath. It was a warm afternoon with a light breeze blowing through the yard. The fragrance of roses and honeysuckle filled the air.

We sat quietly for a few moments. She understood I needed to go home for a while, and then asked what I was going to do.

I said, "I don't know what I plan to do in the distant future, but I know what I've got to do now. I keep thinking of the thousands of dead men buried on dozens of battlefields. Some graves are lost forever; some remains will be plowed up by some farmer, someday; some can be identified and their remains can be shipped home; and many thousands whose bones were compacted together with others in huge common graves will have a solitary marker reading – 'unknown'."

There's a host of other reconstruction and cleaning up that will need to be done as a result of all the folly and foolish destruction war can bring. Unsupervised soldiers allowed to forage for themselves can cause untold amounts of damage on reckless forays around the countryside. I know; I took part in some of it."

I put my arm around Mary and held her close. She took my hand in hers and clasped it tightly as we swung back and forth in the porch swing.

"The war's not really going to be finished for good, for me, until I get this out of my system, and all the dead, or all we can find, have at last gone 'home' for good, too. One happy thought in all this, Mary, is the fact that we will be working out of Washington on this task, and I can see you often."

Mary smiled and said, "I can understand the way you feel, By. You know I love you and I'll be here for you."

"I love you, too," I said, and kissed her for a long time. I walked out through the garden, stopped at the gate and waved.

"I'll be back," I said.

The Story Will Continue In A Future Volume

A Bucktail Company

9 781889 332444